The
Picking Bag
Ammon's Journey Home

The Picking Bag

Ammon's Journey Home

Tom —
Thanks for all you
did to help with
"The Picking Bag"!

Debbra Beecher Nance

Debbra B. Nance

Summary: Alone on a westward trek across the frontier in 1846, a thirteen-year old Mormon boy learns to forgive his absent father, to grieve for his dead mother, and to find faith in his God.

1. Coming of Age- Juvenile Fiction, 2. Mormon Pioneer National Historic Trail—Juvenile Fiction. 3. Frontier and pioneer life- Fiction. 4. Mormons- Fiction. 5. Mormon Church History- Nauvoo- Fiction.

ISBN-13: 978-1-5232-6596-1
ISBN-10: 1-523-26596-5
Library of Congress Control Number: 2016900452
CreateSpace Independent Publishing Platform, North Charleston, SC

Cover Design & photo enhancement courtesy of
    Tom Sjoerdsma, www.artattackgreetings.com
Picking Bag photo courtesy of
    Margaux Kent www.pegandawlbuilt.com

This book is dedicated to my grandchildren

"Never give up,

for that is just the place and time the tide will turn."

Harriet Beecher Stowe

Chapter 1

1846
Nauvoo, Illinois

I was itching to get outside. Sums and reading were well enough, but not on a day when the sun shone bright and it was unusual warm. I tapped my fingers on my slate to the rhythm of a tune that bounced along inside my head. As soon as Brother Pendleton allowed, I collected my hat and scarf from the peg by the door and rushed outside to fresh air and freedom.

I joined my best friend, William. "Let's go to the river."

"My thoughts exactly." William adjusted his black felt hat. "Pa let my older brothers have the afternoon off work and I said I'd meet them after school."

"Do you think the ice will be solid enough for sliding?"

"We'll soon find out." My sister interrupted us when she tugged on my vest. I ignored her, but she kept at it. "Go on home, Sariah. I'll come in time for chores."

"You have to stop by the Post Office, Ammon," Sariah said in her little girl voice. "You promised Ma you'd check for a letter."

"Alright, but don't pester me." I sighed. I *had* promised Ma and Aunt Caroline. I'd have liked to neglect the chore for one day since no letters ever came, but a promise was a promise. "Go on ahead, William, I'll meet you later."

"Don't be long. It'll be dark soon."

I shifted my rucksack onto my shoulder and trotted toward Main Street with its stone sidewalk and half dozen storefronts. I went direct to the Post Office, which was on the ground floor of the newspaper building. I didn't hold much hope of there being a letter. Ma had been waiting months without any word from Pa.

The smell of fresh printers' ink greeted me as I opened the door. A woman untied a packet of letters and spread the mail out on a table set next to a cupboard full of cubbyholes. She looked up from her work. "Hello, Ammon."

"Good afternoon Sister Taylor." I tipped my hat. "Smells like a printing day."

"You are right." Sister Taylor's high-necked

calico dress had an ink spot on the collar, and her hair was falling out of her bun.

"Is there anything for Ma or Aunt Caroline today?"

Sister Taylor picked up a stack of mail and thumbed through it. "I believe there was a letter."

My heart missed a beat. Maybe it was from Pa.

"Not many people send letters in envelopes and pay the postage, too," Sister Taylor said. "Here it is. From Connecticut. Isn't that where your grandmother lives?"

"Yes, Ma's mother." My heart went back to normal as I placed the letter inside my school book. Still no news from Pa. Then I remembered my manners. "Thank you kindly, Ma'am. Ma will be pleased."

"How is your mother?" Sister Taylor asked.

"She still has a bad cough." I twisted my hat in my hands. I hated that everyone asked me if Ma was better. Seemed some folks thought we only needed more faith and she'd get well, but Ma had more faith than anybody else I knew.

"Maybe warmer weather will help." Sister Taylor smiled and went back to her sorting. "Please tell her hello from me."

"I will. Thank you again for the letter." I turned to leave.

"Ammon—wait!" Sister Taylor called after me. "Here's another letter. It's from your pa!"

"From Pa?" I echoed and let the door close.

"Look," she held it up. "It was tucked in with these magazines."

"Is there a black line around the edge?"

"No," she said, "You can rest easy, no bad news."

"Good!" I reached for the letter.

"There's no black line." Sister Taylor pulled her hand back. "But there's no stamp either. You know the rule. The postage must be paid before I can give mail to you."

"How much?" I asked and felt my face flush because I didn't have any money.

"The postmaster marked the price here." She pointed to the letter. "Twenty-five cents. Cash only, remember."

"I'll be back." I opened the door and ran.

"Slow down!" A man called as I dodged folks coming from the Boot Shop.

"Excuse me!" I kept running and turned east on Parley Street then sprinted the last blocks for home. I pushed passed the white picket gate. I leaped the front steps and opened the door, breathing hard. "Ma, Aunt Caroline!"

Jacob reached for me. "Ammon, I been waiting for you."

I dropped my book, hat, and scarf by the door, grabbed my little brother and swung him around the sitting room. Jacob squealed with delight.

"What is it?" Aunt Caroline came to meet me.

4

"Watch now—don't knock over the chair." She wiped her hands on her apron and pushed a stray lock of brown hair back into her bun.

"Ammon?" Ma called feebly from her sickbed in the corner of the kitchen.

"We have a letter from Pa!" I set Jacob down.

He grabbed Sariah's hand, jumped up and down, and chanted. "We got a letter. We got a letter."

"Please." Aunt Caroline put her hand on Jacob's shoulder. "Let go of your sister's hand and calm down. Let Ammon tell us what happened."

"Sister Taylor didn't see the letter at first," I said, "and we have to pay the postage before she'll give it to us, but it didn't have a black line around the edge so it's good news."

"Thank heaven." Ma put a trembling hand to her mouth. "I knew your pa would write."

"Ammon, how much is the postage?" Aunt Caroline asked.

"Twenty-five cents, cash only."

Sariah gasped. "The price of a letter is a . . . a mortification!"

"Yes it is, dear." Aunt Caroline chuckled. "Where did you hear such a big word?"

"I read it in the newspaper." Sariah's face turned scarlet. "You can buy two chickens for twenty-five cents."

"The price was marked right on the letter," I said, "so it can't be helped."

"I'll get my money purse," Aunt Caroline said and left the room.

"Ammon, please get the picking bag." Ma touched my sleeve. "Maybe we can sell the extra buttons for a few pennies."

I lifted the rectangular canvas bag by its long handles from under the table by Ma's bed and carefully turned it upside-down. Ma's sewing supplies and cloth she was saving for a quilt top fell onto her lap. She searched through the scraps to find the buttons strung on a piece of heavy thread.

"You can put those away." Aunt Caroline returned and handed me some coins. "I've got forty-seven cents."

"Will Uncle David be angry if you spend it?" I asked.

"David will understand how important my brother's letter is," Aunt Caroline said. "Besides, this is left from my wages when I taught the common school last fall. Go on, Ammon, get the letter. Don't delay any longer!"

My feet fairly flew as I raced to and from the Post Office and handed Ma the letter. Her fingers shook when she broke the wax seal on a single piece of folded paper.

"August 28, 1845." She read aloud then coughed.

"My, it took almost five months to get here." Aunt Caroline picked up her knitting and sat at a kitchen chair to listen.

Sariah and Jacob were on the end of Ma's bed and I knelt on the floor, reading over Ma's shoulder. Ma spoke slowly. "My Dearest Jane, Brother Matthews and I traveled to the city of New York as we'd planned. We took rides with other travelers when offered, but truly we walked most of the way. We worked for board and room as needed and in this way reached our destination in safety. We preached the gospel of our Lord whenever we could and enjoyed a measure of success."

Ma coughed again and I wanted to snatch the letter from her hand and read it quick. I resisted and soon she continued, "We arrived three weeks ago today and have since been helping a group of saints who recently arrived from Great Britain. Jane, I miss you and the children dearly. I trust you are all doing well. Give Jacob a hug from me and tell him I will be thinking of him, especially on his fourth birthday, Wednesday next. I expect he'll be a fine young man when I return home."

"Hear that Jacob?" Aunt Caroline asked. "Your pa did remember your birthday."

"Tell Sariah, I have seen three newspaper offices and none are finer than our very own right there in Nauvoo," Ma said.

"I must tell Brother Taylor." Sariah smiled.

"Hush, Sariah, let Ma read," I said. "We need to know when Pa will come home."

"Tell Ammon I miss his music and look forward to hearing him play his flute when I return."

Ma coughed, longer this time. She held out the letter to me. "You finish son."

I glanced at Ma's pale face, but took the letter. Pa's handwriting was small and to save paper he'd written horizontally across the page and then crossways in the other direction. I had to decipher his words. "Jane, I must tell you of a most curious turn of events. Since meeting the saints from across the ocean, I have felt compelled to seek out my father's relations. I feel a need to share the gospel with them. This was not part of my plan, but a scripture comes to mind: *He shall plant in the hearts of the children the promises made to the fathers, and the heart of the children shall turn to their fathers. If it were not so, the whole earth would be utterly wasted at His coming.*"

I turned the letter sideways to continue. "My dearest Jane, I asked Brother Pratt about this matter and he has given me leave to sail to Great Britain. Brother Matthews will accompany me and we will help the saints there while I search out my family."

I looked up from the page. "Pa has family in Great Britain?"

"I don't understand," Sariah said. "We're Pa's family."

"Isn't Pa coming home?" Jacob buried his head in Ma's lap and began to whimper.

"Keep reading, Ammon," Aunt Caroline said.

I patted Jacob with one hand and cleared my throat. "We have secured passage on the ship Hood, which leaves in two days. I must depend upon

Caroline and David to help until I can return to you, my dear wife. I expect that will be in late February, which should allow us ample time to complete our preparations to go west with the saints. Tell David to run the shop for me and I will make things right with him when I return. Give my love to all. And please, Jane, forgive me for not writing often. I pray each day that God will watch over and protect you and the children while I do His work and until I return. I remain faithfully yours, James."

I turned the letter over hoping to find more, but that was the end. I felt like someone had punched me in the gut. "Pa left on a ship instead of coming home."

Ma took the letter from me and pressed it to her heart without speaking.

"Don't let us be gloomy." Aunt Caroline put down her knitting. "It's been months since James wrote this letter and he said he'd be home in late February. Today is the 29th of January. He could be home in four weeks, maybe less."

"It is good news." Ma smiled. "We can hope."

"We should celebrate!" Aunt Caroline pushed the chair back to the kitchen table. "Ammon, if you will take Jacob with you while you do your chores, Sariah can help me put some dried apples and apricots to soak. We'll use some of our sugar and make two pies for supper."

"I'd be pleased to help," I said. "Come on, Jacob. You can feed Patch."

It was long past supper. The pies were eaten. Chores were done, scriptures read, and prayers said. I hadn't gone to the river to meet William, but he'd understand. What a glorious day it had been—we'd got a letter from Pa! I laid my head on my pillow and closed my eyes. It was then I remembered that I'd gotten two letters from the Post Office that day.

Chapter 2

I slipped from beneath my quilt. The letter from Grandmother was in my schoolbook, I'd left it by the front door in the excitement over Pa's letter. I didn't bother with a candle. I knew my way in the dark and I'd be quick. My feet made no sound as I stepped past Sariah and Jacob, who were asleep side by side on their straw pallets. A bit of light seeped up from below where the door to the sitting room stood ajar. As I went down the stairs, my aunt's and uncle's voices became clear. I hesitated. Ma said it wasn't polite to interrupt.

"We need to wait for James," Aunt Caroline said firmly. When I heard Pa's name, I sat on the bottom step. A lamp set on Ma's side table reflected light into the oval mirror and lit up the scene. I could see the carved bookshelf Pa had made and the work table with Aunt Caroline's knitting, a piece of yarn dangled toward the braided rug on the floor.

"It may not be safe to stay here any longer." Uncle David's face creased in a frown. He undid the top button of his shirt collar.

"Please—" Aunt Caroline held up her hand. She'd let her hair down and looked young next to her husband on the settee. "Speak soft so we don't wake the children."

I should have gone to bed when I heard that, but I couldn't help myself and leaned forward to listen instead.

"You know the trouble in Lima last fall," Uncle David said, "the threats haven't stopped. Yesterday, John Crawford had a horse taken from his farm by three strangers carrying guns. The men told John to clear out or change religions or they'd be back to burn him out."

Aunt Caroline gasped. "Is he all right?"

"Yes," Uncle David said, "but John has changed his plans. He hired a man to sell his farm. He's taking his family back to Genesee County."

"Back to New York?" Aunt Caroline asked.

Uncle David ran his hand through his sandy colored hair. "They'll leave within a few days."

"It's beginning again, David, the same as when we were in Missouri. The church's enemies thought when they killed the Prophet Joseph we'd all go away; and when we didn't." Aunt Caroline's voice faltered.

"The mob newspapers cause it with their

exaggerations and lies." Uncle David hit his fist into his other hand. I could feel anger in his words.

"Joseph said we'd have to move where the Saints could be alone," Aunt Caroline said.

"Caroline, I think you and I should go back to Genesee County, too."

"We've been assigned to our Company for the journey west. Let's go with the saints. It won't be much longer. Brother Brigham has a group of pioneers ready to go ahead to find places to camp and put in crops."

"You don't understand." Uncle David stood and paced. "There's a rumor the government won't let Mormons leave the states. They're afraid we'll join with the British and start another war. Some people want Mormons on a reservation like Indians."

"They can't do that!" Aunt Caroline's eyes widened. "Can they?"

"I don't know." Uncle David knelt in front of her. His shoulders sagged. "I don't want to fight any more. I don't want to face more mobs. Let's go back to New York and live in peace."

"What about James and Jane and the children?" Aunt Caroline took Uncle David's hands in hers. "What about our beliefs?"

He bowed his head and whispered, "If this is God's church, why hasn't He protected us?"

"God's people have always been tried. It's after that the blessings come. The Lord will provide." Aunt Caroline stroked his hair. The moment was so intimate, I looked away.

"I don't know if I have that kind of faith anymore," Uncle David said. "I'm going out, don't wait up."

I'd never heard that kind of talk—someone questioning his faith. I watched Uncle David pull away, pick up his hat and without looking back walk out of the room. I shivered in the darkness when I heard the front door open and shut. I didn't know what to make of the situation. If Pa were here, I'd have asked him.

Before I could study it out further, the door to the stairs opened. Aunt Caroline stood before me with a candlestick in her hand. She stopped short when she saw me.

"What are you doing out of bed?"

"I . . . I was going to get my schoolbook," I said. "I forgot that another letter came for Ma. I didn't want to interrupt you and Uncle David so I sat down and waited."

"You know better than to listen to a private conversation." The candlelight revealed Aunt Caroline's cheeks were wet with tears. She wrapped her shawl tighter around her shoulders and turned back into the sitting room. Her voice sounded small in the semi-darkness. "I wish you hadn't heard your uncle and me. But now you know our world is falling apart. I told your pa I'd help while he was on his mission and I intend to keep my promise."

Her voice grew louder, "I want our family to go west with the saints. The Lord will take care of us if we have faith."

I wanted to say something—to do something—to feel the resolve my aunt did. "I'll help you," I said going to her. "I'll work harder. I promise!"

"That means a lot to me." Aunt Caroline smiled. "I hadn't realized how tall you've grown. My, you're looking more and more like your pa."

"Thank you." I squared my shoulders. "Now, I'll get that letter for Ma. It's from her ma in Connecticut."

"It's too late tonight, your ma is already asleep," Aunt Caroline said. "Besides, a letter like that can wait. You know how Grandmother Carter can aggravate your ma."

"I hadn't thought of it that way," I said and went back upstairs to my bed.

Early the next day, I lay awake on my straw pallet. Important thing, fearsome things, were happening in Nauvoo. I wished again that Pa were home. He had always made things right. I remembered what Aunt Caroline said about me looking like him and smiled. Pa's hair was darker than mine, but we both had the same brown eyes and long legs. I was near grown up at thirteen. Men started apprenticeships at my age. Before he'd left, Pa had begun to teach me to build cabinets, chairs and other furniture. I wanted to learn more. I had me a good carving knife but I'd need my own set of tools. Pa would help me get them when he got home. In the meantime, I meant to keep my promise to Aunt Caroline.

With that thought, I pulled on my clothes and said my prayers. It was still dark when I went downstairs to build up the kitchen fire. Uncle David had already left for the carpenter shop. After I milked the cow and fed Patch and the chickens, I brought in an extra load of wood and stacked it by the hearth. While I blew on my hands to get warm, I noticed my schoolbook by the front door.

I took out Grandmother's letter. Maybe I should know what it said. After all, Ma didn't need to worry when she wasn't feeling well. I carefully broke the wax seal. Grandmother's ornate script filled the parchment.

December 27, 1845. Dear Jane, When I received the letter stating that your health had declined and that James had left you to go on a mission of all things, I knew what I must do. It is time you realize the mistake you made when you married that man. I don't know how he could leave you in Nauvoo in such conditions. Perhaps, dear Jane, he doesn't intend to return.

My jaw dropped. How could Grandmother write such a thing?

You must come to your senses and give up that fool religion. You and the children must come to live with me in civilization here in Connecticut. Please do not resist me in this matter, Jane. I shall arrive the last week of January, while the roads are frozen and it is easier to travel. I insist—

A sound from the sitting room startled me and I stuffed the letter into my pocket. Aunt Caroline walked into the kitchen. "You're up early. Are your chores done?"

"Yes." I tried not to look guilty and hurried to set the dishes for breakfast.

Aunt Caroline sliced bacon into a pan over the fire. She nodded toward the curtain that divided Ma's bed from the kitchen. "Where's that letter? I'll give it to your ma when she wakes."

I pulled the crumpled page from my pocket and offered it to Aunt Caroline. "I remembered what you said so I read it to see if it would bother Ma."

"Ammon." Aunt Caroline took the letter. "What has gotten into you? I didn't mean to suggest you read your ma's mail."

"I know. I'm sorry, but listen—Grandmother is coming to take us away."

"What are you talking about?" Aunt Caroline mixed cornmeal, buckwheat and water to make small balls.

Sariah came into the kitchen still in her nightclothes and stocking feet with a quilt wrapped around her. "What did you say?"

"Grandmother wants us to live with her since Pa's away," I said. "She sent a letter saying as much."

"I wonder how she knew your pa was gone." Aunt Caroline flattened the cakes of dough and put them to cook in the hot ashes in the grate.

"I have no idea." I shook my head. "I didn't think she and Ma corresponded."

"I wrote to her," Sariah said.

"What?" I said, "Why'd you do a silly thing like that? You know Grandmother hates us Mormons."

"I'm sorry," Sariah said. "Brother Pendleton said writing letters is a good way to improve penmanship. He let me borrow his good pen. I didn't know it would make trouble."

"That is enough, you two." Aunt Caroline gave Sariah a hug and glared at me over her head. "Your grandmother wants to be in control, that's all. She's a rich old woman who gets her way most of the time. She was angry when your ma and pa got married, and she never forgave them when they moved away."

"She said Pa wasn't coming home," I said.

"Don't you worry what she said; your pa will come home," Aunt Caroline said.

"Pa's coming home?" Jacob came into the room dragging his blanket behind.

"Course he is, sleepyhead." I helped Jacob sit up to the table then turned the ashcakes with a fork to cook on the other side. "We're not quite sure when, is all."

Aunt Caroline poured fresh milk into our tin cups and put the bacon on a plate, pouring the grease into a saucer to save for later use. "Your grandmother came to Nauvoo years ago, before

Jacob was born. It was before I'd met David. I was helping your pa and ma with you two." She pointed to Sariah and me.

"Nauvoo was only a handful of cabins set in the middle of a few trees and a big swamp. We lived out of our wagon box. Some of the saints lived in tents, some had nothing and crowded in wherever they could find." Aunt Caroline retrieved the ashcakes and sat at the table. "Let's eat while it's hot. Jacob, it's your turn to bless the food."

After the prayer, we ate in silence. I finished off two pieces of bacon, three ash cakes, and poured myself more milk. "She wore a black hat. Grandmother did, when she came to visit."

"That's right, she always wore a hat." Aunt Caroline helped Jacob cut his ashcakes. "She begged your ma then to go back to Connecticut with her."

"Was that when we were sick?" I asked. "I remember the Prophet Joseph put his hands on my head, prayed for me and I felt better."

"Yes," Aunt Caroline smiled. "Brother Joseph had a great day of blessings. He blessed many that were sick with fevers and they all recovered."

Sariah began to stack the empty plates. "Brother Pendleton said the saints worked together to drain the swamps, plant crops, and build houses."

"He's right," Aunt Caroline said. "You could hear the sounds of hammers from morning to night."

"You can still hear the sound of hammers." I

wiped my mouth with the back of my hand. "Only now people are building wagons to leave."

Aunt Caroline sighed. "That's enough talk this morning. I'll help Jacob wash, and Sariah, I'll braid your hair when you're dressed." Aunt Caroline turned and handed me the letter. "And you better give this to your ma."

Chapter 3

I didn't want to tell Ma that I'd read her letter. I hoped she'd still be asleep when I peeked behind the curtain, but she opened her eyes. Her paper thin skin looked gray next to her white nightdress. Her brown hair was plaited into two long braids that reached below her shoulders. "Hello, Ammon," she said in a raspy voice.

"Morning." I moved the curtain out of the way. "May I help you?"

Ma nodded and I helped ease her into a sitting position. Moving made her cough. I handed her a handkerchief and kept my hand on her back until she stopped. I noticed a tinge of red on the hanky, which she quickly hid.

"How is my young man this morning?" she asked as I helped her lie back against her pillow.

"I . . . I did something wrong."

I avoided Ma's eyes and straightened the quilt then knelt beside her bed. "What with the excitement yesterday, I forgot that another letter came for you... then I read it."

"I do believe you have your father's eyes." Ma ran her finger down my cheek and brushed my hair out of the way. She started to cough again, doubling over. When she stopped, she asked, "Who was the letter from?"

"Your mother. She knows you haven't been well." I couldn't bring myself to say she wanted to take us back with her to Connecticut. Ma was silent for a while. "She's coming to Nauvoo."

"Time was when I'd have been worried to have her here. I'd have wanted to impress her, but not now. Let her come and think what she will."

I looked at Ma closely. I noticed some grey streaks in her hair. Her response wasn't what I'd expected. Ma relaxed back into her pillow. "It's all right that you read my letter, Ammon. Don't worry about it and go on to school. But first, please tell Caroline I'll rest for a while longer. I'm real tired today."

I nodded and Ma closed her eyes. I watched her breath in and out for a time. I hadn't realized until that moment how sick Ma was. I smoothed out the letter from Grandmother and placed it on top of Ma's bible on the table by her bed and went to find Aunt Caroline.

As I walked to school, two things became

clear to me: I did not want Grandmother Carter in Nauvoo, I had no intention of going anywhere with her.

School began as usual with the reciting of lessons. We were interrupted by a knock at the door. A man came in and talked softly with Brother Pendleton, who then raised his hand for silence. Brother Pendleton tugged on his vest and straightened his tie. "Some of you may know that the School Trustees met last evening. Brother Carlson is here to make an announcement."

"The decision has been made to end this school term early," the visitor said. "No doubt your parents told you that we, that is, the saints— will not wait to complete the interior of the Temple and its dedication before beginning the journey west. The Brethren informed the Trustees this morning that the first Company of Hundred is to depart in a matter of days."

The room erupted as if a cannonball had been fired. I whooped and hollered along with my classmates. The time was finally here! The first company would begin in a matter of days. William grabbed my arm and I could see the excitement in his eyes.

"We're going west!" we said together.

In the commotion, one of the youngest girls began to cry. "Calm down children," Brother Pendleton clapped his hands. "Return to your seats at once so we may resume our lessons."

"Thank you, sir." Brother Pendleton ushered the man out the door then turned to us. "The Trustees will inform your parents that today is the last day of our school. Now then, we shall finish the recitations, tidy the room, and stop for dinner recess. You may then go home or stay until the usual dismissal hour."

Brother Pendleton sighed and leaned against the lectern for support. He took a handkerchief from his pocket and mopped his forehead. "I must say, closing the school early has taken me by surprise."

As soon as Brother Pendleton dismissed us for recess, I pulled Sariah aside. "Take my things home and tell Ma and Aunt Caroline the news if they haven't heard. I'll go to the shop to tell Uncle David."

"All right," Sariah said, "but I want to see what the newspapers are going to print."

"There'll be time for that later." I handed Sariah my rucksack, pointed her toward home and gave her a gentle shove.

William joined me outside. "I wondered when the day would come for us to start west. I hope our Company is one of the first to leave."

I nodded. "I wish Pa were here."

William cleared his throat and looked down at the ground. "You expect him soon though, don't you?"

"Yes. We hope from his letter that he'll be

here soon," I said. "I better go find Uncle David and see if he needs help with the shop. Do you want to come?"

"I must go home first," William said. "If I can, I'll walk over to your house after supper."

I hurried toward Pa's carpenter shop. It was near the Temple, high on the bluff overlooking Nauvoo. When I got to higher ground I sat for a few minutes to think about what was happening. I loved this view. All of Nauvoo was spread out below me. The streets were laid out in four-acre squares. Some of the houses were red brick, but most were whitewashed frame or log. Fences surrounded gardens where hundreds of fruit trees would bloom again when spring arrived. I wondered, would we still be here? Farther away on the north and south, I could see where crops had been planted in previous years.

The city of Nauvoo was like a beehive, alive with people coming and going everywhere below me. I could see the Mississippi beyond. During the past summer, steamboats—over a dozen a day—had stopped at the two landings in Nauvoo. But now, where it wasn't frozen, the river flowed sluggishly and pieces of ice pushed against each other.

I turned and looked at the Temple behind me. It had grand white walls carved with sunstones and moonstones, blue star-windows and a bell tower. It looked like a beacon on a hill for all to see. It was beautiful! The Temple stood for everything we saints believed and now we would leave before it was dedicated.

"A matter of days," I said aloud and wondered exactly what that meant. I kicked a small stone and watched it roll down the hill.

From my pocket, I retrieved an ashcake left from breakfast that I'd wrapped in a cloth and wolfed it down for my dinner. I then took out the flute that Pa had made for me. I played a lively tune and let my mind wander. Uncle David had his wagon and some supplies, but there was a list of things that we still needed. I'd heard him and Pa discuss selling the shop and the house to pay for what we'd need. Pa needed to get home in order for us to leave with our Hundred. I wondered for a moment if Ma would be well enough to travel when our turn came. Then another thought hit me: what about Grandmother Carter? She was already on her way to Nauvoo. I leaped to my feet and ran toward Pa's carpenter shop. I had to tell Uncle David the news.

The last few months, Uncle David had begun making barrels for those preparing to go west. Business was good. In fact, he had so many orders, he'd hired extra help. When I got to the shop, Uncle David wasn't there, but one of the workers said he'd return soon. I didn't wait. I walked up the street looking into the various stores. I finally saw him coming from Mulholland Street.

"Uncle David!" I hurried to catch up. "Did you hear the news about the first Company leaving?"

"Yes, Ammon," Uncle David said gravely. "That's why I went to talk to Mr. Morgan. A year ago he told your pa he knew a man that wanted to buy our shop. But now he said the man's offer is only half what it was before."

"What will we do?" I matched my uncle's stride.

"Wait for your pa to return, I suppose."

"I have more news," I said. "Ma got a letter and Grandmother Carter is on her way to Nauvoo. She could arrive today."

"Come again?" Uncle David stopped and looked at me.

"Ma got another letter yesterday that I forgot about," I explained. "It said Grandmother Carter is on her way here to take Ma, Sariah, Jacob and me back to live in Connecticut with her."

Uncle David let out a low whistle. "We'd better get home. I can already see trouble brewing between your grandmother and my Caroline."

A black carriage with runners and a horse stood in front of our house. There weren't many carriages in Nauvoo due to the rough roads. Most folks walked or rode horses. This carriage could mean only one thing: Grandmother had already arrived.

Chapter 4

As I stepped through the door behind Uncle David, I heard a woman's stern voice say, "I think it is for the best."

An older woman dressed in black with matching gloves and a fancy hat with a feather sat on a kitchen chair pulled near Ma's bed. She turned. "Mr. Davis, I believe?"

"Mrs. Carter." Uncle David removed his hat. "How was your journey?"

"It was as expected, long and tiresome. This is Doctor Phineas Granger, my personal physician and surgeon." Grandmother indicated a tall man who stood next to Aunt Caroline. "I persuaded him to drive me here to collect my daughter and her children."

The men shook hands, and Grandmother

asked, "Who is the young man behind you, sir?"

"It's me. Ammon." I stepped around my uncle.

"My, you have grown, Ammon. You're almost a man," Grandmother said. "Come here and kiss me."

I moved forward as commanded and kissed her wrinkled cheek.

"There's a good young man." Grandmother patted my arm. "Now, take your brother and sister upstairs and keep them occupied while we adults take care of some important matters down here. You may begin to pack if you wish, although that will not take long by the looks of things. I want to leave for Connecticut within a day or two."

I looked at Aunt Caroline and she nodded so I took Jacob by the hand and glanced down at Ma. She looked small and weak with her eyes closed, lying still beneath her hand-stitched quilt. She was dressed in her nightdress with her hair in braids. She must have stayed in bed all day. I headed for the stairs. Sariah followed carrying the picking bag.

Once upstairs, Sariah gave the picking bag to Jacob and he sat on the floor in near silence counting and matching the buttons. Sariah and I lay down with our ears pressed flat to the floor in order to hear what was happening below us.

"Jane needs her humors restored to their proper balance," Grandmother said.

"Whatever that means," said Aunt Caroline.

"It is done by bloodletting, which is the proper procedure in this case," a man's voice said calmly.

"That may be your opinion, Doctor Granger," Aunt Caroline said. "But I dare say our own Doctor Lyon might disagree. In my opinion, bloodletting is nothing more than medieval torture. It is a medical practice that I believe should be abandoned."

"Listen to me, young woman." Grandmother's voice rose. "You will step aside and let the doctor do what he must. He is trained in the best-known medical procedures of our day. Jane is *my* daughter. She is in poor health and it seems that she has not received the attention she needs in order to improve."

I could almost see Grandmother's harsh face. "Jane is no relation to you, girl, except through her no account husband, who at this time is nowhere to be found. As I understand, you and your husband have lived here with my daughter, in her home, due to her generosity and kindness since your brother's departure. I assure you that situation can be remedied."

I heard Aunt Caroline gasp. But before she could say another word, I heard Uncle David say, "Mrs. Carter is correct, Caroline. We have no rights in this matter. I believe it is time for us to take a walk. Good afternoon to you, Mrs. Carter, Doctor Granger. "

I heard the back door open and shut.

Sariah sat up. "Who is right, Ammon?"

"I don't know," I said, shaking my head.

"When Grandmother's doctor first came, he gave Ma medicine for her cough. It had a strange wicked-sounding name. Laudanum, I think. It made Ma real sleepy." A tear ran down Sariah's cheek. "I wish Pa was home."

"Me, too." I put my arm around Sariah to comfort her. After a moment I said, "I can't sit here and do nothing. I'm going to find Doctor Lyon and ask him who is right. Sariah, you watch Jacob until I get back."

Quietly, I took the stairs two at a time. I peeked around the corner of the sitting room. The curtain was pulled partway around Ma's bed but I could see Grandmother sitting with her back toward me. She was watching Doctor Granger who had a small knife which he pressed to the inside of Ma's arm. I could see blood drip from the wound, and I heard a moan as I let myself out the front door.

I jumped our white picket fence and ran toward Lyon's Pharmacy. Nauvoo didn't have many doctors. Most folks used home remedies or patent medicines. The newspapers advertised cures for everything from colds to cancer but Ma and Aunt Caroline never bought them. We usually traded with Doctor Lyon for his medicinal herbs when we needed them.

I rounded the corner on Hotchkiss Street and

almost ran into Doctor Lyon as he came out of the Sessions' small home.

"Whoa, Ammon!" Doctor Lyon caught me by the arm. "What's your hurry?"

"Doctor Lyon, you have to help me, sir." I breathed hard. "My grandmother came to Nauvoo and brought another doctor. I think he's killing Ma."

"Ammon, slow down," Doctor Lyon said calmly. "Come inside with me and tell me all that's happened. I am quite sure no doctor would hurt your mother."

I followed Doctor Lyon past the herb garden into his pharmacy and store. Behind the large counter, Sister Lyon stood on a stool and straightened bolts of ready-made cloth. "Good afternoon, Ammon," she said.

"Good afternoon, Ma'am." I nodded.

Lyon's Pharmacy was one of the largest stores in Nauvoo. I noted the barrels of flour, tea, sugar, salt, and other staple foods stacked against the walls. There were also vegetables, wool, flax, hand-sewn clothing and a few animal pelts for sale.

Lately, I'd come many times for herbs for Ma, but I'd never been to Doctor Lyon's home. I followed him up the stairs now to a sitting room above the store.

"Please sit down," Doctor Lyon said. "Tell me exactly what happened."

I told him about the laudanum, the knife, and the blood.

"Your grandmother's doctor has the care of your mother's health now. I will have little say in matters," Doctor Lyon said. "He has already given her the laudanum and probably completed the bloodletting procedure. However, if he is a man of reason I should be able to talk with him and perhaps sway his thoughts about further treatments. If you want, I will come to speak with him this very evening."

"Yes, please." I breathed a sigh of relief. "Thank you."

It was after supper when Doctor Lyon came as he'd promised. Sariah, Jacob and I were told to go upstairs while the adults visited. As I walked to the stairs, Doctor Lyon caught my eye and winked. I closed the door from the sitting room to the stairs but I sat on the steps again so I could hear what happened.

Uncle David made introductions and then Doctor Lyon said, "Your patient seems at ease, Doctor Granger."

"Laudanum does bring comfort, and, of course, I did bleed Mrs. Blakeslee to restore her humors." The casual way Doctor Granger spoke of his treatment for Ma made me cringe.

Doctor Lyon asked, "Could I interest you in joining me for a drink at the tavern to discuss her condition?"

"Yes, of course," Doctor Granger said. "That is, if Mrs. Carter will not need my assistance. Mrs.

Blakeslee is asleep now and should not require anything further for a few hours."

I heard Grandmother murmur her consent and then Doctor Granger said, "I am always interested in discussing a case with someone in our profession."

"Brother Davis, would you care to join us at the tavern?" Doctor Lyon invited.

"No, thank you," Uncle David replied. "Caroline and I plan to visit the Crawford's this evening to tell them goodbye as they leave for the state of New York tomorrow."

I sucked in my breath. Uncle David had been right about the Crawford's leaving.

"Very well, perhaps another time," Doctor Lyon said politely.

I heard Uncle David and Aunt Caroline say their farewells and depart.

"I must warn you, Doctor Granger, Nauvoo is not like other towns," Doctor Lyon said. "Indeed, it is, as they say, 'dry,' as no spirituous liquors are sold here. It is against the law, except that is for medicinal purposes. I assure you, however, that we have other refreshments to offer."

"How unusual, especially for a frontier town," Doctor Granger said. "You must tell me more about your fair city."

"It would be my pleasure. Perhaps you would care to see my pharmacy? I dispense herbs and am what you might call a botanic physician, using natural remedies."

I was surprised at how pleasant Dr. Lyon was being to Grandmother's doctor. But then I heard the two men say their good-byes to Grandmother and I hurried up the stairs so I wouldn't get caught listening again.

Chapter 5

Grandmother called us to the sitting room. "I would like to get to know you better since you will soon be living with me," she said. "Let us sit here and you can tell me about yourselves and about Nauvoo. Things have certainly changed since I was here last."

"Sariah can tell you about Nauvoo," I said. "I'll go sit with Ma."

"I'm sure Jane will be fine with us in here," Grandmother said. "I am hopeful that she will feel better tomorrow. Please stay."

"Thank you just the same," I said. "I'll go sit with Ma."

"Decide for yourself." Grandmother took Jacob's hand and pulled him onto her lap. "Come here Sariah," I heard her continue, "tell me about yourself. Do you attend school?"

I pulled back the curtain from around Ma's bed and moved a kitchen chair close. I sat still and watched Ma, propped against her pillows. Her eyes were closed and her face was deathly pale. I hadn't heard her cough for several hours, but her breath seemed shallow. After a few minutes, I took out my flute and blew softly into it. The delicate melody seeped into my skin and began to soothe my body and mind.

"That was lovely," Ma whispered.

I glanced over and saw her watching me. I smiled. "How do you feel?"

"Better," she said. "I have no pain, but it is sometimes hard to breathe." Ma struggled to sit up higher and I helped her.

"Is your grandmother still here?"

I nodded. "She's in the other room with Jacob and Sariah. Did you know she wants us to go live with her in Connecticut?"

"Yes. She told me," Ma said.

"I don't want to go."

"It might be a good idea Ammon, especially if your pa is delayed. That way Caroline and David can complete their obligation to us and move on with their lives."

I didn't want to consider that possibility so I changed the subject. "Did you know the first Company of saints is to start west soon?"

"Yes, Sariah told me . . . . Ammon, I don't think I'll be going west," Ma said simply. "I think my time on earth is almost finished."

"Don't say such things." I took Ma's hand. "This new medicine will cure you."

"My sweet boy." Ma patted my hand. "You are my oldest and I must tell you, in truth, I feel it is too late for medicine."

"Then we'll ask Uncle David to give you another priesthood blessing—that will cure you."

"No, Ammon. I'm tired. I feel the Lord is calling me home…my body can't last much longer. I hope I can live until your pa returns. I want to tell him how sorry I am for getting sick while he was gone and I want to tell him one last time how much I love him."

I squeezed Ma's hand again as she continued, "With your grandmother here I can rest."

My throat tightened. I knelt beside Ma's bed and wished with all my heart that Pa was home.

"Ammon," Ma whispered. "Promise me something."

"Anything, Ma." My voice cracked.

"If I die before your pa gets home, promise me you will tell him for me."

"Ma, please don't talk this way." I felt tears come to my eyes. "You can't die! I don't want you to die."

"All will be right." Ma's eyes glistened. "God is over all things."

"But, Ma—"

"Hush now, Ammon." She touched my

cheek. "Everyone has to die sometime. It's part of the plan." She spoke slowly. "I'm not afraid to die. I'll go ahead and wait for you. I'll watch over you and my other sweet babies . . . and someday, we'll all be together again."

She smiled and brushed away my tears. "We won't talk of it anymore. Our faith will keep us strong. Please, Ammon, play me another hymn."

I did as Ma asked. I played and Ma listened. Music filled the air and, for a time, everything seemed right with the world. Ma's breathing finally relaxed and I saw she had fallen into a peaceful sleep.

I carefully drew the curtain around Ma's bed so as not to wake her and went outside to get a drink of water. I sat on the edge of the well and thought for a long time about Ma. A sound from the carriage-house pulled me into the present. I had chores to do. Pa had built the carriage-house in hopes we'd get one someday, but then we'd turned it into a stable for our cow and horse, Patch. I opened the half-door and walked inside. I liked the smell of fresh hay mixed with the musty smell of animals that greeted me.

"Hey, boy," I stroked Patch's nose and noted the darker markings around one eye and on his legs that led to his name. Patch was an appaloosa and was to be paired with Uncle David's horse to pull their wagon west. Our wagon was to be pulled by oxen, we had yet to purchase. I talked softly to Patch while I brushed him down and fed him. I told him about

Ma getting worse and about Grandmother's arrival. Patch neighed softly as if he understood. I loved that old horse. I knew if Uncle David and Aunt Caroline left before Pa got home, they'd take Patch with them. I wished we could all go west together as we'd planned before Pa left for his mission.

"Hello, Ammon." William's voice interrupted my thoughts. He wore his black felt hat as usual. "Whose carriage is that out front?"

I explained everything to him while I milked the cow.

"How can you stand your pa being gone, your ma sick, and the saints fixing to leave all at the same time?" William asked.

"What do you mean?

William replied slowly, "Now that it is actually time for us to go west, I wonder if we should."

"You sound like my uncle with your doubts." I poured some water for the cow.

"I know folks say the gospel is true," William said. "But is it worth leaving everything we know? Besides, do you know for sure it's true?"

I thought a while before I answered. "I believe it is true because Ma and Pa taught me to believe." I forked some fresh hay into the stall for the cow. "I think Joseph Smith knew for sure though, for himself."

"We're almost as old as Joseph when he had the vision," William said. "But I haven't had any visits from angels or miracles happen to me."

"Have you prayed for any?" I asked, only half joking.

"No. Have you?"

"No." I answered seriously. "But I believe miracles happen when needed—like blessings that make folks feel better, those are little miracles. And I don't think it takes a vision to know what's true. I can pray to God and ask what's true and I expect the answer will come as a feeling deep inside or from reading the scriptures. Then I'll know. Anyway, that's how Pa explained it to me."

"Ammon, I don't mean to be disrespectful," William said. "But I wonder ...about your pa going to Great Britain and all. Is there any chance your grandmother is right about him not coming home?"

Before I could reply, Sariah came into the carriage-house. "Ammon, Aunt Caroline and Uncle David are back from the Crawford's. We're ready for scripture reading and prayer."

William and I said a hasty goodbye and I followed Sariah into the house. Later that night I lay awake thinking about William's question. Would Pa come home?

Chapter 6

The days dragged by. It seemed everyone else in Nauvoo was packing and preparing to leave. Not us. I did my chores, checked for letters, and worked at the shop with Uncle David while we waited for Pa to come home. On February 6th, I took a rest from making barrels and William and I walked down Parley's Street to the ferry landing. The Millers were readying their six wagons to cross the river on a flatboat, one wagon at a time. It was a slow process.

"Did you see that old sign with the crossing rates posted on it?" William asked.

"Yes." I picked up a stick and broke it in half. "Seventy-five cents for a one horse wagon, twenty-five cents for a yoke of oxen, twelve-and-a-half cents for a foot passenger. That's a lot of money."

"I heard my pa say that Police Chief Stout is

in charge of getting everyone across the river. I don't think he'll charge the regular fares." William stamped his feet to keep warm.

We stood in silence, watching the flatboat push away from the landing. I finally asked William the question I had been avoiding all day. "When do you leave?"

"Pa and my brother got the canvas for the wagon tops today. After the tops are made, we'll be ready."

A line had formed of people and wagons waiting for their turn to cross the river. It looked to me like the flatboat would be busy for a long time.

William continued, "Pa says we'll go when it's our Company's turn."

I felt a twinge of envy. If only my pa would get home, our family could start to pack, and maybe Ma would get better.

As usual, we did no work that Sunday. All of us, except Ma and Grandmother, spent several hours at church services. Our meals were simple and we read from the scriptures together at home. Later, Uncle David and I went to hear Brigham Young speak in a public meeting held on the second floor of the Temple. I heard Brother Brigham say that he and the other Brethren and their families would leave soon for a camp in Iowa about eight miles away called Sugar Creek. He hoped that would ease tensions on this side of the river with the enemies of the Church.

He encouraged all of us saints to prepare to join him across the river, although, a few men were specifically assigned to stay behind to finish the interior so it could be dedicated.

Even though many leaders would be leaving, I felt encouraged that some men were staying to work on the Temple. Surely Pa would be home before the Temple was dedicated and then we could join the camp of saints at Sugar Creek.

About a week later, I heard that Brigham Young and his family had crossed the river and gone to Sugar Creek. Uncle David told me that Brother Brigham planned to return a few times to pray in the Temple, but I knew that the saints' exodus from Nauvoo had truly begun.

And Pa still wasn't home.

Ma was right. With Grandmother in Nauvoo, Aunt Caroline and Uncle David prepared to go west with our assigned Company. Uncle David closed the shop, storing Pa's tools in the carriage house. I never heard him or Aunt Caroline say any more about going to New York.

I helped them pack their wagon with sacks and barrels of flour, cornmeal, beans, smoked pork, dried fruit, vegetables and other supplies they'd need. They didn't say goodbye yet, but Uncle David hitched up Patch and his horse and drove the wagon to take a place in line for the flatboat. While waiting, Aunt Caroline stayed at home and visited with Ma every day.

Once when Ma was asleep, I heard Grandmother and Aunt Caroline talking. "My dear, I have come to see you in a different light." Grandmother patted Aunt Caroline's cheek. "I thank you for your kindness in caring for my daughter and her children."

"You're very welcome," Aunt Caroline said. "I hope you will also believe James. There are a few days yet before the end of February. Please be patient, Mrs. Carter. I know my brother. He will come home and then he'll want his family to join the saints at Sugar Creek."

"I trust now that your brother intended to return," Grandmother said. "Still delays happen and Jane has not responded to the medical treatments of my surgeon or your doctor. I think our best course is to get her and the children to New Haven with me. I have a nice home and servants there who can care for her. We shall wait for James until the end of the month, but no longer. The journey will only become more difficult the longer we wait."

I went outside and sat down behind the smokehouse. I'd known Ma wasn't getting any better but I hadn't wanted to admit it. I picked up a pebble and threw it at the leafless apple tree in the corner of the lot. I couldn't forget what Grandmother had said before about Pa. Why wasn't he home? Pa could make things right. I knew he could.

The temperature dropped that night. It was the 23rd of February and the river finally froze solid.

It was bitter cold the next day. Aunt Caroline and Uncle David came and said their goodbyes. They took the cow and tied it to the back of their wagon. Sariah and I walked with them down to the river.

We watched Uncle David urge the horses onto the frozen riverbed. The wagon shuddered as it slid down the side of the bank and hit the ice but then it steadied and they were on their way.

"Goodbye," Uncle David called.

"God keep you safe until we meet again." Aunt Caroline waved.

"When will that be?" I muttered as I took Sariah's hand and walked toward home. Then a familiar black felt hat came into view. William was in line with his family to cross the river.

"Look at that," William said. "The line is moving much faster now that we can simply walk across the river."

"We never had a chance to slide on it this year." I blew on my fingers to warm them.

"No. Though we knew it would freeze solid sometime. It freezes every winter," William said.

"Not usually overnight," I replied and adjusted my woolen scarf to cover my ears.

"Some folks say it's a miracle," Sariah said.

William and I looked at her and nodded. Then he asked, "Any word yet from your pa?"

"No, and you saw Aunt Caroline and Uncle David are on their way to Sugar Creek. They felt like they needed to go with our Hundred."

"Sugar Creek is only eight miles away," William said.

"It might as well be a thousand." I replied.

Chapter 7

After the river froze and Aunt Caroline and Uncle David left, Ma got worse. She didn't get out of bed anymore. Doctor Granger gave her more medicine that allowed her to sleep most of the time, but her cough returned.

A few nights later, Ma's cough woke me and I sat up against the wall. Grandmother was a silent sleeping mound in the bed where Aunt Caroline and Uncle David used to sleep. Sariah and Jacob were also asleep on their mattresses. I heard Ma cough again, so I tiptoed downstairs. Doctor Granger had made a bed in the sitting room to be near Ma. It was empty. I looked around the corner and found the doctor sitting by Ma, holding her hand. A lamp, made of a round piece of paper folded to the center and pinched to a point and placed on top of a saucer of grease, glowed softly on Ma's table. It would burn all night.

Dr. Granger looked up. "Hello."

"I couldn't sleep," I said. "I heard Ma coughing again."

"Come here, my boy," Doctor Granger held out his hand and then shifted his chair to make room for me. "It's been a hard day for your ma. Her lungs are forced to work ever harder. Consumption is a terrible disease."

I sat on the floor by Ma's bed. "Is that what she's got?"

"I'm afraid so." The doctor covered me with part of his blanket and then kept his hand on my shoulder. "I've spoken at length with Doctor Lyon, and . . . Ammon, doctors don't have the means for helping some people. I wish we did. I'm not of your faith, but I've seen many things. One person lives at great odds while another passes on when they should have lived. I believe we all have our time to die. I'm sorry, but I believe your ma's time is very short. We must leave it up to the Lord now."

I didn't know what to say. I sat quiet and rested my hand on Ma's. When my eyes got heavy, I leaned my head against the carved wooden bedpost and slept. I woke a few hours later. I was cold and stiff. The blanket Doctor Granger had given me had slid to the floor. He was wrapped in another blanket, sitting in the chair, softly snoring.

I put a log on the fire in the kitchen and went

back to my place next to Ma. I looked at her in the firelight. She looked beautiful in her sleep—like what an angel must look like. I watched her breathe for a while and then touched her hand. Her eyes fluttered open and she smiled at me.

"I love you, Ammon." She took a little breathe. "Don't forget your promise."

She didn't breathe out. I waited, but Ma didn't breathe out or take another breath. I shook her hand. But she didn't move. Her face of a sudden turned grayer and I knew Ma had gone where I couldn't follow.

"I won't forget, Ma," I whispered and then I bowed my head and wept.

I walked between Jacob and Sariah behind the wagon that carried Ma's simple pine coffin. Jacob clutched the picking bag tightly to his chest as we walked toward the cemetery.

"Do you want me to hold that for you Jacob so it doesn't drag on the ground?" Aunt Caroline asked. She and Uncle David had come back from Sugar Creek for Ma's funeral. They walked behind us with Grandmother, Doctor Granger, and a few family friends.

"No," I answered for my little brother. "It makes Jacob feel close to Ma to hold her picking bag."

We were a sad group moving slowly down Durphy Street. Grandmother was the only one dressed in all black; none of the rest of us owned mourning clothes. The fact that I had known people in Nauvoo who died from illness or accident didn't make it easier for me to face my own mother's death.

I stood with Sariah and Jacob near the open grave where Ma's wooden casket would be laid. I listened to the words Uncle David said. They were meant to encourage, inspire and give hope to those of us left behind.

They didn't help.

I felt empty . . . like there was nothing left inside. Jacob clung to me and cried when the first shovelful of dirt hit Ma's coffin so I picked him up and held him tight. Sariah leaned her head against my arm. Whatever would we do without our ma?

After the services, we walked home in silence. Friends and neighbors came by to visit and bring food. They talked with Grandmother, Aunt Caroline and Uncle David. Plenty of folks offered kind words to me, but I didn't really hear them. Jacob fell asleep on the sofa with his thumb in his mouth and his head on Sariah's lap.

I put more wood on the fire in the kitchen grate and noticed Ma's bed, empty in the corner. It didn't seem right. I pulled the curtain closed around it and went outside. I wanted to be alone. The air was cold and felt good. I went behind the smokehouse and sat next to Ma's favorite apricot tree. I remembered how she'd taken special care to water it when it was first planted. I remembered, too, how she used to sing while she washed clothes, made bread, sewed or worked in her garden.

The words to one of her favorite hymns went through my mind. "God, our help in ages past, Our hope for years to come, Be thou our guide while life shall last, And our eternal home."

I knew Ma had believed while her life lasted. I wondered if I believed. I took my flute from my pocket and began to play Ma's hymn. I thought about the night I'd played my flute for her and the look of peace that had come on her face. I kept playing her hymn. Over and over, I wanted to fill the empty place in my soul. The music didn't help this time. There was nothing inside me, not even tears.

William came around the corner of the smokehouse. "Here you are. I heard your music," he said and sat down beside me. "I'm real sorry about your ma."

I didn't trust my voice to reply so I nodded. We sat in silence for a time.

"What will happen now?" William asked.

"Grandmother says there's no need to wait any longer for Pa to come home." My voice sounded hoarse. "She doesn't want any of Ma's furniture either and told Aunt Caroline and Uncle David to do what they want with it. Uncle David volunteered to follow us as far as the steamboat landing in Ohio to make sure we get there safely. He's going to take a wagonload of furniture to sell there, too, since no one is buying that kind of thing anymore here. We're supposed to leave tomorrow. Aunt Caroline will go back to Sugar Creek with friends."

"I hoped you would come to Sugar Creek with your aunt instead of going to Connecticut," William said.

"I wish I could," I said. "But Grandmother won't allow it."

"What about Patch?"

"Aunt Caroline will keep him," I said.

"It seems strange. You and I are both leaving everything we know to go to places we don't know anything about." William picked up a stray piece of hay. "I hope we see each other again."

"I'm sure Pa will come home soon and he'll come to get us," I said a little too loudly.

"Of course," William replied. "I didn't mean….Then you'll join us in Sugar Creek."

"Yes, I believe so." I forced a smile. "We'll join up before too long."

"Let's don't say good-bye." William dropped the piece of hay and extended his hand.

"Agreed." I shook his hand. "We'll see each other soon enough."

"If you ever need anything," William's voice trailed. "If your grandmother treats you mean, come and find me."

"I'll do that," I replied.

I sat beside Doctor Granger as he drove the carriage with Grandmother, Jacob and Sariah inside. Uncle

David followed behind, his wagon piled with furniture. I had my flute and my carving knife in my vest pockets. Sariah had Ma's bible and some writing paper. Jacob had the picking bag and a wooden horse Pa had carved for him. Grandmother said she'd buy us whatever else we wanted or needed when we reached New Haven.

All I wanted was to be home.

I was quiet as we drove past the houses in the flats. Then we went up the road past the Temple and the shops on the bluff. I didn't allow myself to think that this might be the last time I'd see Nauvoo and the Temple that I loved.

"I think you'll like where we're going, Ammon. It is by the ocean." Doctor Granger said amiably. "I'll be glad to get back to my wife and son."

"I didn't know you had a family," I said.

"Yes. My son is about Sariah's age. I hope you will be friends."

"I don't mean to be disrespectful, sir, but I do not want to live in Connecticut."

"You may speak freely, Ammon. I'll not take offense." The doctor clicked his tongue to keep the horse moving.

"If Grandmother would let me, I'd be with Aunt Caroline in Sugar Creek. Sariah and Jacob would be too. If I could, I'd go back right now. I want to be in Nauvoo or nearby when Pa returns. I promised to tell him something for Ma."

"I'm truly sorry your pa didn't get home before we left."

"I dreamed about Ma last night," I said as if I hadn't heard. "She was well and strong and happy. She sang her hymn as we walked beside our wagons. All of us–Aunt Caroline, Uncle David, Pa, Ma, Sariah, Jacob, and me—we were headed west with the saints. It was a good dream."

The doctor was silent so I said. "I know that dream can't come true, but I think we're going all the way to Connecticut for nothing. Pa will come for us and then we'll turn around and go west with the saints."

"It will be hard for your pa now that your mother is gone," Doctor Granger said gently. "It'll take him some time to adjust. It may be a while before he can come to Connecticut for you."

"That may be true." I paused to think for a minute. "But I'll help Pa. We will be all right."

"Ammon, you must remember Sariah and Jacob are young," They still need a woman's care."

"Aunt Caroline could be a ma to them."

"That would be up to your aunt and uncle, and your pa," Doctor Granger said. "I'm sure your aunt loves you very much but she is young herself and she'll want a family of her own with her husband. Sometimes things don't work out how we want. I understand your wish to go west, but your pa will need to consider many things before he decides what is best for your family."

Chapter 8

We stayed the night at an inn at a crossroads some twelve or fifteen miles east of Nauvoo. I'd never stayed at an inn before and under different circumstances I might have enjoyed it. Grandmother ordered our supper and made arrangements for rooms, one for herself and Sariah, and one for the rest of us.

I couldn't settle down. I lay thinking long after everyone else was asleep. I knew what Doctor Granger had told me was true, but that didn't change how I felt about going to Connecticut. Careful not to wake Jacob, I edged out of the bed we shared and went next door to Grandmother's room. I carefully opened the door a crack and peeked inside. Moonlight shone dimly through the window where the curtains didn't meet.

Grandmother, in her white lace bonnet, was asleep on a big brass bed with her back toward the door. Sariah was on the near side of the bed. I wondered how I would wake her, but she must have heard the door. She opened her eyes and sat up when she saw me. I motioned for her to come and she climbed out of the bed.

Grandmother began to stir so Sariah whispered. "I'm going to the 'necessary' house. I'll return directly."

"Use the chamber pot," Grandmother mumbled but then she began to snore.

Shivering, Sariah reached for her woolen scarf from the end of the bed and wrapped it around herself as she crept toward me.

"We need to talk," I whispered in her ear. "Come on, before we wake Grandmother." I closed the door carefully and we felt our way along the dark hallway toward the main dining hall where we had eaten supper earlier. The fire in the hearth was banked with glowing embers. I pulled Sariah to a wooden bench by the table farthest from the kitchen.

"Sariah, I've decided to go back to Nauvoo."

"What are you talking about?" Sariah's voice was loud.

"Hush!" I motioned for her to be quiet and whispered, "I don't want to go to Connecticut with Grandmother. I'm going back to wait for Pa."

"Ammon, none of us want to go with Grandmother," she hissed between her teeth, "but

57

how can you—"

"I've decided," I interrupted. "I'm going back to wait for Pa. The longer I stay with Grandmother, the farther away I'll be from Nauvoo. I have to go back now."

"It's a long way, Ammon, and it's too cold for you to go tonight," Sariah said. "You'll have to wait."

I was relieved she wasn't arguing with me. "You're right, Sariah. It would be better to go tomorrow morning. I'll leave after we eat breakfast."

"Are you sure you can walk back to Nauvoo?" Sariah asked.

"Yes. I'm going back," I said. "Besides, I'll most likely hitch a ride and be in Nauvoo by tomorrow night. If not, I promise that I'll keep moving to stay warm and I'll find a place indoors to sleep."

"Take this." Sariah unwound her scarf and handed it to me. "It will help you stay warm."

The next morning while Grandmother settled the bill, I got my chance. I pulled Sariah and Jacob around to the far side of the inn. "Jacob, I need to tell you something. You must promise not to tell anyone for two whole days." I went down on one knee beside him.

"Is it a game?" Jacob asked putting his small hand in mine.

"No, it is very serious. You see, I must go back to Nauvoo by myself. Pa will be there soon and

I want to tell him what happened to Ma and how the saints have started the journey west. You must be a big boy now and mind Sariah. Pa and I will come for both of you when we can."

"All right, Ammon." Jacob said with complete trust. "I'll be good and I'll never tell where you're going."

"Good." I patted his arm. "Now, Sariah, I don't know how long it will be before Pa and I can come for you. Promise that you'll take care of Jacob. Help him say his prayers and tell him stories every night."

"I will." Sariah bit her lip to stop any tears.

"We'll be good, Ammon," Jacob said. "I'll pray for you and Pa."

I got a lump in my throat and hugged them both. "I have to go now." I stood to leave.

"Wait, Ammon!" Jacob tugged on my hand. "Take this." He held out the picking bag with Ma's sewing things inside.

I hesitated. "But Jacob, you said it made you feel close to Ma to hold it."

"You need it more than me," he said. "I have Sariah."

"Take this, too," Sariah held out Ma's bible. "Grandmother will buy a new one for us in Connecticut."

I took Ma's bible and slid it into the picking bag. I hugged my sister and brother again. "Thank you. I'll take good care of these things and give them back to you when Pa and I come for you."

Sariah took Jacob by the hand and they walked toward the front of the inn. I hoped they would keep Grandmother distracted. I waited until I was sure no one would see me and then I ran to the inn's stables. Once inside, I quickly hid in one of the stalls behind a couple of barrels. I scrunched down on the ground against the back wall and covered myself with straw. I could see part of the stable doors from where I was hidden. My heart pounded against my chest. What would happen next?

I heard voices outside. Apparently, Grandmother had discovered my absence. "Where is that boy? Have either of you gentlemen seen him?"

"Not since breakfast." I heard Doctor Granger reply.

"Not me either," Uncle David said.

"What about you two?" I heard Grandmother demand. "He can't have disappeared."

I couldn't hear Sariah's reply, but I heard Jacob's high-pitched voice. "We promised not to tell."

Bless him, I thought, smiling. Jacob might be little, but he was good to his word. Grandmother wouldn't learn anything from him.

"We must find Ammon," Grandmother said loudly.

"I'll speak with the innkeeper," Uncle David said.

"I'll look in the stables," Doctor Granger

added.

When I heard the stable doors open, I sat as if frozen in place, hardly daring to breathe. Doctor Granger called, "Ammon, are you in here?" I could hear the crunch of his shoes against the straw and I could see him look around in the various stalls. I held my breath as he came nearer.

"Ammon?" The doctor moved still closer. I saw him bend down to look at something in the straw. About that time, I realized I didn't have the picking bag anymore. It must have slid off my shoulder in my rush to hide. The doctor stood up and, sure enough, he was examining the picking bag. Looking around he hesitated for a moment. Then he placed the bag on top of the barrel next to where I was hiding. He started to leave and then turned back.

"Good luck to you, Ammon. I hope your pa is there when you get back to Nauvoo. If not, go straight to your aunt at the Sugar Creek camp. I wish you God's speed."

Dr. Granger closed the stable doors behind him and I was alone.

"The boy is not going to be found here." I heard him call to Grandmother. "Perhaps he ran off as soon as breakfast was finished."

I brushed off the straw, surprised and happy with my good fortune. Dr. Granger was not going to tell Grandmother where I was. It seemed a sign that God was blessing me to return to Nauvoo to find Pa. I hurried to the stable doors to better hear what was happening outside.

"If we go back to Nauvoo now it may take us hours or even days to find Ammon," Uncle David said.

"He told me yesterday that he wished he could have gone with his aunt," Doctor Granger said. "I believe the death of his mother affected him more than we knew. I should have realized he would try to run away and watched him closer."

"This will not do!" Grandmother said harshly. "Jane's passing has been hard on all of us, but that is no cause for the boy to be disobedient. I must say that I'm somewhat at a loss as to what we should do now. I had hoped we would push on quickly while the weather holds."

"Nauvoo is only a day away," Doctor Granger said. "I'm sure that is where Ammon is headed. I think it best to let him go. It will give him some time to think things through about his mother."

"It would teach him a good lesson, if we left him behind," Grandmother said. "Make him think twice before being disobedient again. I suppose I can hire a man from the inn to go look for him."

"If we bring him back now he'd probably run away again," Uncle David said.

Doctor Granger added, "The good people of Nauvoo will help him until his pa returns."

"Or I'll find him when I go back through Nauvoo and take him to Sugar Creek with me," Uncle David said.

"I suppose you are right," Grandmother said. "My late husband, bless his soul, ran off when he was about Ammon's age and he turned out all right. I suppose Ammon has his Grandfather's will. Then it is decided. We shall let Ammon fend for himself for a time and we shall press onward. Sariah, please help Jacob into the carriage. Doctor Granger, let us proceed as quickly as possible."

I ran to the ladder on the other side of the stable and climbed to the loft where I could see Grandmother's carriage and the wagon pull away. As I watched, Sariah leaned out the carriage window looking back toward the stables and me. She stayed that way until they were almost out of sight and then gave a slight wave and disappeared within the carriage. I had an almost overwhelming urge to yell to her and run after the carriage.

Maybe that is what Grandmother thought would happen. But I took a deep breath, said a quick prayer for strength, and stayed where I was. I had made my decision. I was going back to Nauvoo to wait for Pa. He'd be home in a day or so, I was sure of it. Maybe he'd even be home by the time I got there. Then we'd catch up to Grandmother and get Jacob and Sariah. We could help Uncle David sell the furniture, buy the oxen we needed, and join the saints at Sugar Creek. I retrieved the picking bag, stuffed some straw between my shirt and my vest to help insulate me against the cold, adjusted my two scarves and hat, and began walking toward Nauvoo.

Chapter 9

I walked for several hours without seeing anyone else on the road. My hopes of getting a ride disappeared. Going back to Nauvoo was harder than I expected. As I walked I couldn't help wonder how Sariah and Jacob were getting along with Grandmother. I wondered how far they'd traveled. I certainly couldn't catch up to them now even if I wanted to. No, I'd made my choice. I was going home. I must hope for the best.

Sariah had been right; it was cold. I beat my hands against my sides and alternated running and walking to keep my blood circulating. I put one scarf around my neck and the other around my head and ears. My stomach growled. I wished I had saved a biscuit from breakfast. The road I was walking on was nothing more than two wagon wheel ruts running between clumps of leafless trees, brown bushes, and dead grass, with an occasional farmhouse off in the distance. I kept walking.

When the sun dipped below the horizon and I still had some miles to go, I began to wonder if I'd made a bad choice. I felt a flutter of fear in my stomach. I couldn't make it back to Nauvoo this night. I needed to find a place to sleep. I trotted down the next lane that I came to where in the distance I could see a farmhouse with smoke curling up from the chimney. I removed the straw from between my shirt and vest and hid it behind a bush to use the next day. Then I wiped my face on my sleeve and straightened my hair with my fingers so I'd be more presentable. An old woman with a crocheted shawl around her shoulders and a musket in her hands answered my knock.

"Hello." She set down the gun. "Awful cold tonight for a boy to be out walking, isn't it?"

"Please, Ma'am, I'm on my way home but it's still a long way," I held my hat in my hands. "I wondered if you might help me."

"I'm sure what you'll be wanting is a place to sleep and some food." The woman looked me over carefully. Her face was lined with wrinkles and her dress was faded but I could see the porch was swept clean and she had a kind voice.

"Yes." I said. "Could I chop some wood for you?"

"I suppose, and you can fetch some water

from the well."

I followed the woman around to the back of the house and drew two buckets of water. I carried them to her back door and then started in on the woodpile. The axe I used was old but the blade was sharp and it didn't take long to split a small pile of wood. I could see my breath as I swung the axe in the dwindling light. It felt good to get my blood moving faster.

"That's enough," the woman called from her doorway. "Bring an arm load of wood and come inside."

"Thank you kindly." I put the axe back in its place and picked up the wood.

"My mister's gone to town, you see, to get supplies," the woman lit a lamp as she spoke. "He don't much care for visitors. But he won't be back 'til tomorrow or the next day and I could use some conversation. Set yourself down there and tell me your story."

I stacked the wood by the hearth and told the woman about Grandmother. While I talked, she got me a hunk of bread and a bowl of soup made with turnips and other vegetables. Between bites I told her about Pa's letter and Ma's passing, and how I had to get back to Nauvoo.

"What's that you got there?" the woman asked me as I finished eating.

"It's Ma's picking bag. I've got her bible in it now. And also the cloth, buttons and such she used to save." I rummaged around inside and held up the string of buttons. "I could give you the buttons for the food I've eaten. Do you want to look?"

"No child, you keep your treasures." The woman patted my arm.

"Thank you for the supper, Ma'am," I said. "It was grand!"

"Oh, go on. You were just about to die from lack of food, is all." She beamed. "Now, let me understand your situation. You're walking by yourself back to Nauvoo to find your pa."

"Yes Ma'am."

"Are you one of them Mormons?"

I nodded. I wondered what she knew of Mormons and if she would still let me stay the night.

"Good thing my mister ain't home. He's not too fond of Mormons, but they've always been good to me. When I was younger, you see, I had a baby die, a boy. He'd be older than you, but anyway, a neighbor-lady came to help. She was Mormon. She brought food and cared for me. She said some nice things about my boy. Said I would see him again in heaven. I never forgot."

"I won't forget you either, Ma'am," I said, and I silently thanked God for that kind neighbor-lady, wherever she was.

"You can sleep in there." The woman indicated a small room off the kitchen. "That's where the hired help and travelers sleep in the summer. It will be cold so I'll get you a blanket."

I thought for a moment about reading my scriptures like we used to do at home. But then I lay down on the cot with the picking bag for a pillow, I was asleep before the old woman returned.

In the morning I huddled under the blanket for a while, trying to get warm. The sun wasn't up yet so it was at the coldest time of day. My legs felt stiff and I was bone tired from walking. I thought about my family and wondered where they were now. When I heard sounds coming from the kitchen, I forced myself to get out from under the blanket, said a quick prayer, and went to warm up by the fire.

The old woman made ashcakes for breakfast. She gave me a hunk of cooked bacon and a couple of ashcakes to take for my journey as well. I thanked her and started down the lane to retrieve my straw.

"Boy," she called after me. I turned and she held out the blanket she'd let me use. "Take this, you might need it."

I smiled and tipped my hat. "Thank you ever so much, Ma'am. I appreciate all you've done for me."

I put the blanket around my shoulders and soon I was on the main road walking toward Nauvoo. I took out my flute and played a quick tune as I walked. Everything was going to be fine. I was headed home.

After a few hours of walking I ate the leftover bacon and ashcakes. I thanked the Lord again for the kindness of the woman who had given the food to me. Two wagons passed going away from Nauvoo, but there were none going my way. By early afternoon I was hungry. I decided to go to another farmhouse and ask for food in exchange for work.

I saw a place in the distance that looked promising. I turned off the road and walked toward it. But before I got there, I heard a dog snarl. I crept forward and saw a skinny woman come out of the house carrying a rifle.

"What do you smell, dawg?" she called. "Go get it." Then she bent down to untie the struggling dog. I didn't wait to see if what the dog smelled was me. I turned and ran until I was far enough away to feel safe. I sat for a few moments to rest but it was still cold, so I got up and walked on. My feet were beginning to hurt and my stomach growled. It had been hours since I'd eaten and I really needed water. Again and again I repeated to myself that I'd made the right choice and I kept walking toward Nauvoo.

I came to the top of yet another small rise and there above the treetops, I could see the tower of the Temple. How it shone in the late afternoon sun! I smiled in relief. I was almost home.

I jogged for awhile and then slowed to a walk when I crossed Barnett Street. I was looking at the Temple tower and nearly bumped into two ladies as they came out of a shop on Mulholland Street. "Pardon me." I tipped my hat and slipped inside the open door.

Unnoticed, I made my way to the stove in the corner of the store. I sat on the floor with my back against a barrel of beans and looked around the dim interior. Though I hadn't been here before, it was similar to the shops down on the flats. I recognized the distinctive odors mixed together of leather, wood, spices, and molasses. Holding out my hands to the stove, I felt its warmth begin to spread through my body and began to relax. Three men sat at a table nearby. They were loudly discussing some point of politics. I paid them no mind until a turn in the conversation caught my attention.

"I heard a man from Quincy say if all the Mormons aren't gone before summer, there'll be hell to pay," one man said.

I looked up at that and studied the men. I didn't know them. But I could tell by the clothes they wore that one was a shopkeeper and the others were farmers.

"Morgan, you know hundreds have already left. I think the rest will follow," a second man said.

"They will if they know what's good for them." The third man chuckled.

"They kept their pledge not to plant spring crops. That shows they mean to leave," the second man said. "It doesn't help that no one will buy their property."

"Why buy it?" The man called Morgan laughed callously. "We can have it for nothing soon enough."

I didn't hear the rest of the conversation because a woman came over to me. "I'm Mrs. Morgan, the proprietor's wife. May I help you?" She had been arranging a display of seed packets and had apparently noticed me.

"No thank you, Ma'am." I stood to leave. "I was getting warm is all, but I'll go now."

"What's your name?" she motioned for me to follow her.

"Ammon Blakeslee."

"Blakeslee, you say?" Mrs. Morgan walked back to the counter.

"Yes Ma'am." I moved closer.

"That name sounds familiar." She pulled out a large box and leafed through it. "Ever since the Post Office on Main Street closed, the mail gets left here. Letters that aren't picked up are put in this box. Yes, here's one for Jane Blakeslee. Is she a relation to you?"

"She's my ma," I said eagerly. "Who's the letter from?"

"Let me see," Mrs. Morgan said. "It's from James Blakeslee."

"That's my pa!" I said. "We've been waiting for him to come home. Could I have the letter, please?"

"We have the same rules as the Post Office," she said. "You have to pay the twenty-five cents postage first."

"I haven't got any money," I said.

"I'm sorry. There are no exceptions." She put the letter back in the box.

"May I work for it?" I asked. "I could sweep the floors or put away your stock."

"My daughter helps us in the afternoons when Mr. Morgan and I take our tea. We don't need any other help. Maybe you can ask for work at another shop in town." She went back to the seed display.

I felt desperate and followed her. "Ma'am, would you take my blanket or my flute or my knife in trade?"

She shook her head. "Sorry, everyone leaving Nauvoo has wanted to trade or sell us their sundries. It's cash only for the mail. That's the rule."

I went back to my spot near the stove. I had to think. There must be a way to get that letter from Pa. Only one man, the shopkeeper called Morgan, remained in the store. He sat alone reading a newspaper. Morgan—that name seemed familiar to me. Yes. I remembered now. On the day Grandmother arrived, Uncle David had said he talked with a Mr. Morgan. This must be the same man. I gathered my courage and tapped him on his shoulder.

"Mr. Morgan, sir . . . May I have a word with you?"

"Yes, my boy." Mr. Morgan lowered his newspaper and looked over his spectacles. "What is it?"

"My name is Ammon Blakeslee. I believe my

Uncle David spoke to you a few weeks ago about a man buying our carpenter shop?" I asked.

"Yes. I spoke to your uncle." Mr. Morgan took off his glasses and cleaned them with his handkerchief.

"I wondered..." Suddenly I felt sweaty and I realized I must look a sight, but I couldn't stop now. "Might you tell me who the man is? I was hoping he'd lend me a little money until the shop is sold."

"Why, what do you mean?" Mr. Morgan said pushing back his chair. "Where is your uncle? I thought he'd left Nauvoo."

I could feel my face flush and I didn't know what to say.

"What kind of trouble are you in, boy?" he asked.

"Where's your family?" Mrs. Morgan joined her husband.

"Sorry to have bothered you," I said quickly and ran for the door. "Thank you anyway."

"Wait!" I heard Mrs. Morgan call after me.

I pushed open the door and ran. I didn't want them to ask any more questions. I especially didn't want them to know I was alone. What would they do with me, a Mormon? I hurried past White Street, turned left on Partridge and ran toward home. I looked down Hotchkiss as I passed; no one came or went from Lyon's Pharmacy. Two of the homes and the watch repair shop on Partridge Street were boarded up. It was eerie. As I ran I thought something else was different. It took me a while to pinpoint what it was: Except for the sound of the ice breaking up on the river, Nauvoo was quiet. The sounds of building had stopped.

I hurried to open the gate to our yard. "Aunt Caroline!" I hollered.

Everything looked so familiar that for a moment I'd forgotten she was gone. Everyone was gone. I glanced in the carriage house. It stood empty except for Pa's tools set on a shelf. I slowly opened the door to the house and went inside. Ma's broom stood behind the door and a pile of wood lay stacked by the hearth. I wandered through the vacant rooms. The only furniture that remained was the kitchen table, a chair, and one sleeping mattress. One thing for sure, I was alone.

What was I to do now?

First things first, I went out to the well, drew some water and drank deeply. Next, I used my flint and built a fire. A cloth-covered bundle sat on the table with a letter addressed to Pa beside it. I untied the bundle and found enough smoked meat, ashcakes, and dried fruit to last for several days. Heaven bless Aunt Caroline! She must have believed as I did that Pa would arrive soon. I ate a small piece of the meat and drank another cup of water. The ashcakes had hardened but I soaked one in water to soften and nibbled at it and ate a couple of dried apricots. After finishing, I felt better.

I picked up the letter to Pa. It felt heavy and had a wide black line drawn around the edge. Pa would know for sure there was bad news. The handwriting belonged to Aunt Caroline. I slid my finger under the fold and broke the wax seal. Several coins fell out when I unfolded the page. I counted them—twenty-two cents. It was the last of Aunt Caroline's teaching money. I set the unread letter back on the table. I knew the news it contained and didn't want to read it. I absentmindedly played with the coins. With Aunt Caroline's money I only needed three cents to pay the postage for Pa's letter. Slowly a plan formed in my mind.

At teatime the next day, I watched from a distance until Mr. and Mrs. Morgan left their store together. I waited a minute and then hurried across the street.

"Hello," I said as I entered the store and gently closed the door behind me.

"Hello," a young woman replied as she took off her bonnet and tied on a work apron.

I figured she was the Morgans' daughter and spoke to her as such. "I was here yesterday and your ma said there was a letter for my family. I have twenty-two cents cash for the postage."

"What's the name?"

"Blakeslee."

The young woman retrieved the letter. "The postage is twenty-five cents."

"We only have twenty-two cents in cash." I

held out the coins. "But we have some buttons to trade for the rest."

"Let me take a look," she sounded annoyed.

I turned out the contents of the picking bag onto the counter.

"Nothing worth much here." She looked briefly at Ma's bible and the assorted pieces of cloth and then sifted through the buttons on the thread.

"Please," I pleaded. "We need that letter. It's from my pa."

"Oh, all right." She sighed and gathered up the buttons. "Give me your money and these will make up the difference."

"Thank you." I handed her the coins. "Thank you very much."

I shoved the book and cloth back in the picking bag, took the letter and hurried outside before she could change her mind.

Chapter 10

Ma's name was written across the folded paper. I felt a pang in my heart. Ma should be the one reading this letter, not me. But I couldn't help that now. I broke the wax seal and unfolded the page.

January 1, 1846-

This letter had arrived in two months when the first one from Pa had taken much longer.

My Dearest Jane, We received a letter today from the Brethren informing us that trouble has increased in Nauvoo. I will send this letter by return post. I pray that you and the children are well. I will begin my journey home as soon as I finish the work here.

Pa should have done more than pray for us, I thought bitterly. He should have come home.

Let me tell you all that has happened in the last few months. At first my desire to go to Great Britain seemed to be for naught for I was unable to locate my father's ancestral home. I feared my prayers had gone unanswered and almost gave up hope.

However two days ago, while I waited at a railway station, I met a woman on her way to visit her husband's father. I learned that he is John Blakeslee, my father's first cousin. The very man and family for whom I have been searching! My newfound relation and I had a friendly conversation and I made arrangements to meet her husband and his father.

I shared the gospel with them, specifically the teaching of families being bound together forever and they have accepted this message and wish to be baptized. As soon as this is accomplished, I will begin my journey for home.

I shook my head in disbelief. Pa had stayed too long in Great Britain. I could feel my anger at him grow.

After attending to our matters of business in Nauvoo with regard to the carpenter shop and with David's assistance, I believe we shall be ready to journey west with the saints.

I clenched my fist. Pa was too late. Most of the saints had already left Nauvoo including Caroline and David. I forced myself to finish reading.

Jane, it is such a blessed time to be alive! Is it not? Give my love to each of the children. I trust they are behaving properly and helping you. I am much encouraged since I found my "lost" family. They have expressed a desire to come to America too. I look forward to when we shall all be together as one large happy family!

As always, I remain faithfully yours, James.

I stood still, dazed. So much had happened that Pa didn't know. It was almost too much to think about. I began walking without caring where my feet took me. I came to the place where I'd rested the day Grandmother arrived in Nauvoo and sat down on the ground. I'd been so sure Pa would be home or at least come home soon and make things right. Instead, I had another letter full of words and nothing more.

I felt the same empty feeling I'd had after Ma died, only worse. How could Pa go to Great Britain in the first place? I figured how many days he'd been gone and I realized if he'd come home when we'd first planned, he'd have been in Nauvoo before Ma died. Maybe she would have lived with him here. For certain Grandmother wouldn't have taken Sariah and Jacob away.

Where was Pa now? His letter said he'd found his lost family. That might be true, but in doing so, Pa had lost us, his real family. Ma was dead. Sariah and Jacob were gone. Aunt Caroline and Uncle David were traveling west. And me? I was alone.

All at once, I didn't want to wait anymore for Pa to come home. I'd waited long enough. I crumpled Pa's letter and shoved it in the Picking Bag. I didn't care where Pa was. I didn't want to see him. Let Pa have his *lost* family. I didn't need him or them.

I stood up. What should I do now? The Company of Hundred that my family had been assigned to was long gone from Nauvoo. I wondered if I knew anyone that remained in the city. I remembered there were a few men assigned to work on the interior of the Temple. Surely one of them knew Pa or Uncle David. I could find someone to help me. But then, I didn't want pity and I didn't want to be sent back to Grandmother. I was better off alone. I'd find my way by myself. It was growing dark so I started walking toward home. Home. I no longer had a home.

I ate more of the food Aunt Caroline had left for Pa and lay on the straw mattress that I'd placed near the hearth. I took out my flute and began to play, but the sound gave me no comfort so I put it in the picking bag. I knew Ma would have told me to pray but I didn't want to. I was sure the prayer wouldn't go past the ceiling. I missed Ma.

The next morning I gathered my few possessions and remaining food and walked toward the river. I was going to Sugar Creek to find Aunt Caroline. Chief Stout was no longer in charge of the ferry crossing. I didn't know the new operator or his assistants. I watched as they loaded a wagon onto the flatboat and wondered what the price was to cross the river.

Before I lost my nerve, I walked straight up to the operator and said, "Excuse me, sir."

"The name's Drummond," the man said crisply. "Mister Drummond to you. What can I do for you?" He was a short man with burly arms, red hair and a short beard. When he spoke, he took hold of the collar of his coat with his thumbs and rocked back and forth on to his toes as if he were trying to appear taller.

"I'd like to cross the river, Mr. Drummond" I said. "But I don't have any money."

"That would be a problem then, wouldn't it?" Mr. Drummond pushed his hat back on his head.

"Could I work for you to pay my way?'

"Sorry lad, I have the help I need."

"Would you take my flute in trade?" I pulled it from the picking bag to show him.

"Now, if it were a pipe for smoking, instead of a pipe for making music, I might consider it." Mr. Drummond laughed at his joke.

"Please, Mr. Drummond, I'm on my way to Sugar Creek. I have to find my aunt," I pleaded.

"Have you got anything else to trade?" Mr. Drummond pulled on his beard.

"Not much," I said. "I have a little food, a blanket, my knife, this canvas bag that holds scraps of cloth, Ma's bible, and my clothes."

"You do have a fine looking scarf there." Mr. Drummond fingered the end of it. "Do I see you have two?"

"Yes." I unwound one from my neck. "I almost forgot; my sister Sariah gave me hers."

"And where is Sariah now?" Mr. Drummond asked.

"She's with my grandmother and my brother in Connecticut."

"Now, how did you come to be here when your brother and sister are with your grandmother in Connecticut, and your aunt in Sugar Creek? Where are your parents, laddy?" Mr. Drummond asked.

"I don't know where Pa is," I said. "And Ma… she passed away."

"Sorry to hear that," Mr. Drummond cleared his throat and looked away.

"I need to find my aunt before she moves west." I took a step closer and held out my scarf. "Please, Mr. Drummond, will you take this for my passage?"

"All right then." Mr. Drummond reached for the scarf and wrapped it snugly around his broad neck. "It'll do. Get on board. Find a place out of the way and hold on. With the ice still breaking up, we could have a rough ride."

"Thank you, sir." I climbed onto the flatboat, feeling it sway in the water. I found a place to sit among the barrels and boxes that were lashed to the side railing.

I couldn't help but be excited. I'd never before been on a flatboat. This one was a crudely built craft about fifteen feet wide and long enough for a single wagon, oxen, and some extra cargo to fit stacked along the sides and railings. I watched as the wagon owner and Mr. Drummond talked while the rest of the barrels and boxes were loaded. Then the signal was given and the assistants cast off. We were on our way.

Using long poles, Mr. Drummond and his men pushed the raft out into the murky water. Mr. Drummond used his pole to steer us and to occasionally push away a chunk of ice. As the dark water slid past, I couldn't help remember the newspaper reports I'd often read about the mishaps of river travel. I slung the picking bag over my head and shoulder and held on tight to the icy railing.

The river was about three quarters of a mile wide where we were crossing. When we reached halfway, I began to relax and enjoy the ride. But that didn't last long. The flatboat lurched unexpectedly and tipped to one side. An ox bellowed. I looked around. Something didn't seem right. The flatboat was turning backward in the current. The wagon owner grabbed one of the ropes that held the wagon in place.

"What happened?" I asked.

"Ice!" Mr. Drummond shouted and headed for the side where we'd been hit.

I felt another massive jolt. The wagon jerked and tore loose from the lashings and rolled toward the end of the boat.

"She's tipping!" One assistant hollered.

"Take to the ropes!" Mr. Drummond hollered back.

I grabbed a rope along with the other men. We pulled with all our strength to bring the wagon back to center, but the flatboat tilted more and swirled slowly out of control.

"Hold her!" yelled Mr. Drummond.

"Hah! Move on!" The wagon owner urged the frightened oxen.

But they couldn't or wouldn't move forward. It was like a game of tug-of-war with us against the oxen and the wagon.

As if in slow motion, I watched another chunk of ice slam into the boat. Two barrels broke free and rolled into the water. The raft was beginning to break apart. The wagon rolled backward, dragging the oxen and us with it. I heard the other men's desperate cries and more bellows from the oxen. A spray of cold water hit me in the face and the ropes stung as they pulled through my hands. I tightened my grip, but couldn't stop the rope from slipping.

In a matter of a few seconds, the wagon crashed through the back railing and into the water. The flatboat immediately righted itself, washing the deck with icy water. The oxen, their eyes wide with terror, bawled, and struggled as the weight of the wagon dragged them closer to the edge of the craft. We pulled on the ropes and the oxen's yoke but it did no good. The oxen's back legs slid into the water.

Mr. Drummond hollered, "Cut 'em free!"

It was too late. No one could reach the lines and the wagon was sinking fast.

"Let go the rope or you'll be swept in yourselves," Mr. Drummond called.

We did as he said and watched, helpless, as the bawling oxen's forelegs slid into the water and the weight of the wagon pulled them beneath the water.

I dropped to the deck, my body shaking at what had happened. Mr. Drummond and his assistants got us to the ferry landing and tied up what was left of the flatboat. Cold and exhausted, we hurried to Mr. Drummond's hut by the river. We huddled around a fire one of the assistants had built up in the grate.

"How am I going to tell my wife?" The wagon owner said in disbelief. His hat was gone, his coat torn and his hands burned from the ropes. "I planned to set up camp on this side of the river and go back for her and the children. That wagon held all our worldly goods."

Mr. Drummond dropped his head into his hands. "I'm so sorry."

After a few moments of silence, I whispered, "At least we're alive."

"The boy is right." One assistant said, putting his hand on the wagon owner's shoulder. "You might have lost more. At least you have your wife and children."

"Aye," said the other assistant. "That was a bad one, that crossing was. Mr. Drummond, I think we could do with some whiskey and a bit of food to warm us."

"There's whiskey in that jug on the shelf and

water in that pitcher for those who'd rather," Mr. Drummond indicated. "But I don't have much in the way of food on this side of the river. There may be a bit of bread in the cupboard."

"I have food." I said and quickly shared my dried fruit and meat from the picking bag. I held back two apricots from my small portion to save for later. We ate and talked about the mishap for a while. With some food in our bellies, we even laughed a little at Mr. Dummond's stories of worse crossings. We were happy to be alive, almost giddy with relief, after the accident.

When we were warm, Mr. Drummond said, "You travelers can stay here for the night if you wish. But me and the lads are back to the boat. We'll lash it fast and get across the river before nightfall."

"I'll help," the wagon owner said. "I want to get back to my family as soon as I can." He turned to me at the door. "Thank you for sharing your food, Ammon. I'll pray you find your aunt."

"Thank you, sir," I said. "I hope your wife will understand."

"Things will be fine. We've only lost our wagon. Not our faith or each other."

For lack of anything better to do, I emptied the picking bag and examined its contents. My flute seemed no worse for the ordeal we'd been through. I fingered the wood and put it to my lips. I blew softly, but it made me feel more alone so I put it away. I thought of the wagon owner. He was going back to his wife and family. At least they had each other and their faith. That was Ma's kind of faith. I wondered... did I have any?

Ma's bible was wet on the edges but I hoped it wouldn't be ruined. I set it aside. I found Pa's letter stuck between some pieces of cloth. I wanted to throw it in the fire but then I saw Ma's name and traced it with my finger. Pa should have returned to Nauvoo as he'd promised. Ma had needed him. I had needed him. And now Ma was gone—gone forever. She didn't get the chance to tell Pa the things she'd wanted and now I was supposed to tell him.

I shoved the letter and everything else back in the picking bag. At that moment I hated Pa. I knew I shouldn't, Ma wouldn't approve, but I couldn't help myself. Why hadn't Pa come home like he promised? God should have made him come home. I missed Ma.

It was too late to walk to Sugar Creek now. I sat and watched the fire burn low. At least I had a place to stay for the night. I looked around taking in the details of the hut, its rough log table and bench, straw mattress set against the far wall, and wooden shelf for a cupboard. I wrestled with my thoughts until I gave up and lay down.

When I closed my eyes, I could see the terrified oxen and hear their bellows echo inside my head. When I finally fell into a restless sleep, I relived the river crossing again and again in my dreams. Once I dreamed I fell into the river and couldn't pull myself onto the flatboat. I woke in a sweat with my heart beating fiercely. For a moment I didn't know where I was. Then I remembered I was safe inside the hut by the river. It was night. I stirred up the fire and took deep breaths until I went back to sleep.

Chapter 11

Daylight brought no sunshine, only a steady light rain and a headache. When the rain hadn't stopped by midday, I decided I couldn't wait any longer. I ate the last of my food. Then with my knife, I made a slit in the middle of my blanket, pulled it over my head and put on my hat. I was as ready as I could get so I went out into the storm.

Eight miles is a manageable distance but with the rain and my head hurting, it became miserable. My felt hat sagged after a short while. Mud clung to my boots and made them heavier with each step. The road was little more than a trail made by the hundreds of saints that had left Nauvoo and gone before me to Sugar Creek. Here and there I could see where a wagon had been stuck and dug out of the mud and where folks had cast off pieces of furniture. It made it easy to follow the trail.

After walking a few miles, I wanted to stop and rest but there was no shelter on either side of the trail. I should have waited out the rain in the hut. It was too late to turn back now. I kept walking.

The rain seeped through my blanket and coat. I set my sights ahead to a bush or a curve in the trail and told myself that I only needed to get that far. Then when I got to that spot, I chose a new goal. Time passed and eventually, as I rounded a bend, I saw a few scattered tents in the distance. I wanted to run to them. But by then I was so tired, wet, and cold, I simply didn't have the strength to run.

"Hello the camp," I called in the traditional greeting as I neared the first tent.

A woman opened the tent flap. "What have we here? Come in, boy. You look near drowned."

"Yes, Ma'am," I murmured as I sank to the ground.

The woman hollered for help and someone took my wet blanket and hat and half carried, half dragged me inside the tent. My wet clothes were peeled off and I was wrapped in a quilt. "Thank you," I said, and closed my eyes to sleep.

"Ammon . . . wake up, Ammon."

I stirred. I recognized that voice. "Aunt Caroline?" I sat up and rubbed my eyes.

Aunt Caroline knelt on the floor next to me in her long skirt. She opened her shawl and hugged me to her. "I'm here. I'm so glad you're all right. You had a fever, but you seem better now."

"I was trying to get to Sugar Creek to find you," I said. "How did you find me?"

Aunt Caroline sat beside me. "This is Sugar Creek. You're at the Stones' tent. Sister Stone recognized you and sent one of her boys for me."

"My head doesn't hurt anymore. I'm grateful for Sister Stone letting me get warm."

"Yes, but how did you come to be here? Where are Sariah, Jacob and your grandmother?"

I told Aunt Caroline the details while I pulled on my dry clothes and boots.

"Doctor Granger knew you were in the stable and he left you there?" Aunt Caroline shook her head. "What was he thinking?!"

"Now Aunt Caroline, don't be angry," I patted her arm. "I got to Nauvoo safely." I didn't want to tell her about Pa's letter in front of Sister Stone so I skipped that part and told her about the accident with the oxen while crossing the river.

Aunt Caroline was indignant. "You made it to Nauvoo safely, only to nearly drown crossing the river. If I ever see Doctor Granger again, I'll have something to say to him!"

"I'm here safe now," I said trying to calm her. "Besides I'd have run away again if he'd made me stay with Grandmother."

"All I can say is: thank heaven you're alive!" Aunt Caroline got to her feet. "Can you walk to my camp? It isn't far."

I nodded. "I'm fine now that I'm dry."

Aunt Caroline and I thanked the Stones for their help and said our good-byes. Then I followed my aunt as she picked her way through the trees and around the various wagons and tents scattered about the area.

"I sorely missed you," Aunt Caroline said as we reached her campsite. "It was much too quiet with everyone gone."

"I missed you too." I smiled. "How are things here in Sugar Creek?"

"Perhaps a little harder than I expected," Aunt Caroline said. "You see, when the Brethren first came here some of the saints in Nauvoo panicked. They were afraid they would be left behind. With the river frozen, more and more folks came to Sugar Creek whether or not they were prepared. It was confusing—all Brother Brigham's well-laid plans were forgotten. We shared the food we had, but many of us have used most of our supplies. The Brethren bought some food to help but we'll need more."

"I didn't see many tents or wagons. Where is everyone?"

"The main camp of saints moved to Richardson's Point on the first day of March. We're all to follow as soon as we can."

"Where is Richardson's Point?"

"About thirty miles west of here," Aunt

Caroline said. "We'll go as soon as David gets back. It's a good thing we found you."

The rain slowed to a drizzle and stopped the next morning. I was happy to be with Aunt Caroline and wanted to do my part. I fed and milked the cow, squirting warm milk directly into my mouth. Then I fed Patch and brushed him down. I was happy to see my old friend and talked to him as I had in Nauvoo.

When I finished my chores, I helped Aunt Caroline hang up some clothes and bedding on tree branches to dry. It was then I remembered Pa's letter.

"Aunt Caroline." I went into the tent and got the picking bag. "We got another letter from Pa. I hope you don't mind that I used your money to pay the postage for it."

"That was a good use for the money." Aunt Caroline took the letter eagerly. "Is he well?"

I ignored her question. "I ate all the food you left for Pa, too."

She touched my arm. "I'm glad it was there for you, Ammon. Now, what did your Pa say in his letter?"

"It was addressed to Ma. You should read it for yourself." I avoided looking at my aunt and went to gather wood for the fire.

Aunt Caroline didn't say anything about the letter until after supper that night. "Your Pa didn't say how long it would take for him to get home, did he?"

"No!" I said. "And I no longer care how long it takes. He won't find us there in Nauvoo. He found a new family. Let him stay with them."

"Ammon," Aunt Caroline started, "you don't mean that."

"I do." I clenched my fist. I could feel my throat tighten and tears sprang to my eyes but I swallowed hard. I wasn't going to cry. "If Pa had come home instead of going to Great Britain, Grandmother wouldn't have taken Sariah and Jacob. Maybe Ma would have lived. Anyway, we would all be together right now if Pa would have come home when he promised."

Aunt Caroline pulled me to her. "Your ma didn't want to die, Ammon. But she was awful sick. Don't let your hurt feelings cause you to lose your pa, too."

I thought about that for a moment while I was safe in my aunt's arms. Then I pulled away. I couldn't forgive Pa for not being there when we needed him.

A week later, as Aunt Caroline and I were finishing supper, Uncle David walked into camp. His clothes looked rumpled—like he'd slept in them—and he hadn't shaved for a few days.

"David!" Aunt Caroline cried and ran to him. "I'm so happy you're back!"

"Me, too." Uncle David hugged her. "I stopped by the house in Nauvoo and saw it was empty." Uncle David came over and tousled my hair. "And you, I see you made it to Sugar Creek in one piece."

"Yes sir." I ducked my head.

"Sit down." Aunt Caroline took Uncle David's hand and led him to a log near the tent door. "You must be tired and hungry. I'll get you something to eat while you tell us everything that's happened."

"I'll need to wash up, too, and then you can tell me where everyone is."

While Uncle David ate, Aunt Caroline told him how the Brethren and most of the saints had moved on to the next camp. Uncle David told us about his journey with Grandmother and the others. The frozen roads had made it fairly easy to travel. He had seen them safely to the steamboat in Ohio. He had sold the furniture and then begun the return journey to Nauvoo.

"Thank you for the food, Caroline." Uncle David stretched his legs out. "I am tired."

"Do we need to take care of anything? Where is the wagon?" Aunt Caroline asked.

"Let me rest for a while," Uncle David said. "I have some more things to tell you."

"Of course." Aunt Caroline knelt beside Uncle David. "Let me help you take off your boots. Ammon, please gather more firewood."

"Uncle David," I said when I returned with an armload of sticks. "I saw where you tied your horse. But the wagon was empty. Where are the supplies?"

"That's the main thing I have to tell Caroline and you. I guess it's just as well said now as later. I didn't buy any supplies."

"What?" Aunt Caroline's eyes got big.

"Before you get upset, let me explain." Uncle David pulled Aunt Caroline over to sit on the log next to him.

I sat nearby listening.

"I've had plenty of time to think about this," Uncle David continued. "I want you to hear me out completely before you say anything. I planned to buy the supplies–maybe even get a team of oxen for James. But when I got to Ohio, I asked around and who do you think I met there at the steamboat landing?"

"Who?" Aunt Caroline and I asked together.

"John Crawford. He'd left his family there in Ohio while he went to secure their new place. He'd returned a few days before I got there and had hired out to haul goods with his wagon to earn money for the steamboat fare." Uncle David's eyes were gleaming bright and he talked faster and faster, "John and I talked, and, Caroline, I gave him most of the money I had for the supplies and asked him to get us a stake by his in Genesee County, New York!"

Aunt Caroline's jaw dropped, but she remained silent.

Uncle David didn't notice and hurried on. "I

think this is the right thing for us to do, Caroline. We'll be safe there. We can take Ammon with us. James will come, too, after he goes to Connecticut for the children. I left James another note at the house in Nauvoo so he'll know where to find us."

Aunt Caroline's face had turned pale and she whispered, "What about following the Prophet and going west with the saints?"

"The Prophet Joseph is dead, Caroline. And the Brethren have gone." Uncle David stood up and paced in front of us.

"The church isn't dead, it will continue and the Brethren will lead us. They aren't that far away." Aunt Caroline's voice rose. She reached for Uncle David.

"I've made up my mind," Uncle David said firmly. "I am going to Genesee County."

"Is that so?" Aunt Caroline stood. The light had gone out of her eyes and her face was stern. "I need some time to think, David."

She adjusted her shawl. "Ammon, finish your chores and then go to bed." Aunt Caroline walked away into the gathering dusk.

Uncle David and I looked at each other, speechless for a moment. "Your aunt is a stubborn woman, but she'll come around. Better do as she said."

Later that night, I heard Aunt Caroline return. Uncle David and I had gone to bed but he had a candle burning. They must have thought I was asleep, but I lay in the semi-darkness on my side of the tent, watching what happened.

Aunt Caroline's voice was calm as she spoke softly to Uncle David. "I did as you asked. I thought through what you said very carefully."

He took her hand. "You're chilled to the bone. Come, let me warm you."

Aunt Caroline sat next to him and undid her high-top shoes. "I'm sure you saw we're low on supplies."

"Yes. What happened?" Uncle David wrapped a blanket around her shoulders.

Aunt Caroline explained and then said, "I shared because I thought you would bring more food and supplies, but now we don't have enough for the journey west."

"All the more reason to go east." Uncle David gently pulled Aunt Caroline closer.

"I believe the Lord will provide for those who give freely." She snuggled in next to Uncle David. The moment was so personal I closed my eyes, but I could still hear my aunt's voice.

"The Brethren will lead us in the right way. Some men have gone to find work. You could join them. We could still go with the saints if we use our faith. We only need to get to the next camp."

"Let's talk more about this in the morning," Uncle David said. The candle went out then and they were quiet.

Chapter 12

I woke late and lay on my back for a few moments listening to the rain hit the top of the tent. I could hear my aunt and uncle outside eating breakfast so I pulled on my boots and joined them.

"Good morning, sleepyhead," Uncle David greeted me. We sat under a sort of canvas awning attached to the tent and two trees that protected everything from most of the rain.

"Just in time for breakfast." Aunt Caroline handed me a tin plate.

"Thank you, and good morning." I sat on a log. I didn't want to think about what I'd heard them say the night before and decided to keep the conversation light. "This isn't quite as comfortable as the old kitchen table and chairs, is it?"

"Not quite," Uncle David answered amiably.

"You'll like the new place in Genesee County. Why, John Crawford told me there's a stream that runs through our properties and a pretty little grove of hardwood trees on the southwest corner. It's not far to town and I think we can build a nice home. I hope your pa will join us. We can build a new shop and have a new table and chairs real soon."

"Wait, you already know about the trees on our property?" Aunt Caroline asked. "I thought you said you met John at the steamboat landing and gave him money to find us a place."

"Yes, umm," Uncle David stammered. His face turned red. "I...I guess I didn't tell you exactly right."

"Did you lie to me?" Aunt Caroline glared at her husband. "David, tell me exactly what happened."

Uncle David put his plate down. "I tried to tell you before we came to Sugar Creek the first time, Caroline. I sent the money and a letter to John when we went to Nauvoo for Jane's funeral. I asked him."

"At Jane's funeral?" Aunt Caroline interrupted, her voice rising angrily. "You must have planned things before then, else how did you know where to send a letter? You did lie to me! You made arrangements to buy that property when you knew I didn't want to go. You never did plan to go west, did you?"

"I didn't plan to lie to you. I tried to tell you back in Nauvoo," Uncle David said. "I sold my half of the shop to Mr. Morgan and gave the money to John before he left for Genesee County. Then I met John again at the steamboat landing. I planned for us to follow him long ago, as soon as James returned to Nauvoo. But James never came and Mrs. Carter did. We needed to move out of the house so I brought you as far as Sugar Creek. I thought while I was gone, you'd see that going west is too hard."

"But, David."

"Do you like living in a tent, giving away all our food and supplies?" Uncle David interrupted. "I don't!"

"The Lord will provide," Aunt Caroline began.

"I meant what I said yesterday, Caroline. I've had enough. I will not go west. I am going east to New York." Uncle David picked up his hat and walked out of camp into the rain. "I need to see about buying some supplies."

I looked at Aunt Caroline who quickly turned away and began to clear the dishes. "Is he really going back east?" I asked.

"He seems set on it," she said softly. "The question is, will I go with him?" She went inside the tent.

I looked at the tent door and then after my uncle who was disappearing among the trees. "Wait," I hollered and ran to catch up with Uncle David.

"I'm riled up right now, Ammon." Uncle David had gone to his horse and was tightening the strap on his saddle.

"Will you truly go back to New York? Will you turn your back on our religion?" I shivered in the rain.

"I'll no longer starve or freeze or be put upon by other people if that's what you mean." Uncle David swung into the saddle. "And I refuse to go to an unknown place out west."

"What about Aunt Caroline?"

"I want her to come with me," Uncle David replied. "Ammon, go on back to camp. Your aunt will need your help."

Uncle David returned to our camp in time for supper. Later, he and Aunt Caroline spoke alone in soft tones, which I couldn't hear. I hoped Aunt Caroline could persuade Uncle David to go west. It seemed to me to be the right thing—the only thing to do. If only our whole family were here, I was sure we would go west.

I fell asleep to the steady rhythm of the rain hitting the top of the tent.

The next morning, Uncle David left early but I saw him and Aunt Caroline kiss and she looked happy. When we were alone, Aunt Caroline told me that she had decided to go back to Nauvoo with Uncle David and then on to Genesee County, New York.

"I thought you said Mormons never give up," I said, my voice rising. "That's what you're doing!"

"You don't understand everything." Aunt

Caroline took my arm and made me look at her. "I had not spoken of it before because it would not have been proper, but I'm going to have a child. A child needs his father, Ammon. I must go with David; he is my husband. I still have faith in God and I believe someday David and I will join the saints out west. Until then, I have my faith and we'll live our religion the best we can wherever we are."

I turned my back on her. I didn't want to go back to Nauvoo. I wanted to go west with the saints now.

"Please, Ammon," Aunt Caroline coaxed. "Things will work out, you'll see. Come and help me pack. We'll start back for Nauvoo tomorrow."

I slept badly that night and had jumbled dreams of Pa laughing with his new family, while Ma coughed in the background, and oxen bellowed and clambered to get onto a flatboat. I woke with a start and lay in the dark, letting my heart rate return to normal. Aunt Caroline and Uncle David were on their side of the tent. When I was sure I hadn't woken them, I put on my boots, pulled my blanket with the slit over my head and went outside.

The rain had stopped and faint moonlight shone through the trees. I went to where Patch was tethered and silently saddled him with Pa's saddle. Earlier I had filled the saddlebags with food and supplies without Aunt Caroline or Uncle David taking particular notice.

I took Pa's rifle, powder horn, and the picking bag with the things I'd brought from Nauvoo. I left a note that read: I've come too far to go back now. I'll join the saints and go west with them. Please do not follow.

Patch and I picked our way quietly through the few remaining campsites of Sugar Creek and found the road leading to Richardson's Point. I figured I had three hours before Aunt Caroline and Uncle David would find my note. I hoped they would abide my wishes.

The first day's travel went smoothly. The sun shone brightly, like a promise that spring would come again. I enjoyed riding Patch, especially since I had walked most everywhere in Nauvoo. I pushed any thoughts of family out of my head. I thought only of the journey ahead. My plan was a simple one: catch up to the saints and find my friend William. I'd figure out the rest later.

The trail was muddy with standing puddles from all the rain. Patch was well rested though and easily made his way around and through the worst mud holes. The going was slow. I figured we'd traveled eleven or twelve miles. An hour before sunset, I found a nice place by a stream to stop for the night. I couldn't help but feel good. Uncle David hadn't come after me and I was on my way west.

The next day was worse. Rain drizzled and a harsh wind blew. It was hard to start a fire so my breakfast consisted of day-old ashcakes. The novelty of riding wore off and soon my backside hurt from the saddle. The rain didn't stop and the trail became harder to follow with mud holes larger and closer together. Before long, my hat was wet through and sagging again, which made it hard to see. My headache returned and with it a cough. I knew I should be grateful it was rain instead of snow, but I wasn't. My fingers were stiff from the cold and my toes went numb. When that happened I jogged along the trail for a time.

The sky was dark most of the day, and at one point, I felt obliged to lead Patch because of all the mud holes. When my stomach told me it was past suppertime, I hadn't found a place to make camp. "We can't go much farther today," I told Patch. "It's too dangerous to walk in the dark with all the mud holes. We might as well stop here for the night."

My hat and blanket were wet. My coat, pants and boots were wet. I doubted there was a part of me that wasn't at least damp. I dismounted and dropped Patch's reins. I scanned the area and saw a wagon box with a broken wheel near a boulder on the side of the trail. With Patch's help I pushed and shoved the box until I got it to flip over against the boulder, making a sort of lean to. I ducked underneath the wagon box and found I was protected from the rain and wind. I looped Patch's rein to one of the wagon wheels and took off Patch's saddle.

"We didn't come as far as yesterday," I told him as I brushed him down the best I could with my hand. "Maybe three-and-a-half to four miles is all. It'll take longer to get to Richardson's Point than I hoped."

Patch stamped his foot and tossed his head. I gathered some dead pine needles and brush from under some nearby trees and piled them together in my niche by the boulder. After a few tries with my flint, I got a small flame going. I added more dry needles until I had a nice little fire. The heat reflected off the rock and felt good. I was hopeful I could dry out and I leaned against the boulder. Soon I fell into an exhausted sleep.

I woke up hungry. I stirred the fire so I could see and dug through the saddlebag to find an old ashcake. I drank the rest of the water from my water pouch. I huddled there under my blanket until the sky began to lighten. I thought about staying longer where I was but I had nothing left to burn and decided I needed to keep moving to stay warm.

"There's no reason to stay here," I said to Patch. "Let's get going."

I let Patch drink from one of the larger puddles and gave him a handful of cornmeal from the saddle bag. "Not much of a breakfast, my friend." I rubbed his neck and swung up into the saddle. It felt warm to be back on Patch and I was glad we were together.

After several hours, I was feeling sore again from riding so I got off and walked. My boots became thick with mud. They stuck so fast with each step that it was an effort to walk. My feet pulled up first followed by my boots which constantly rubbed against my heels. This had bothered me a little the day before but I had been able to ignore it. Now my heels throbbed. I could feel blisters forming.

The rain started up again and I was very cold. My cough was worse. I could hardly see the trail, so I climbed back on Patch, closed my eyes and let him have his way. I must have dozed off because I woke with a start when Patch nickered and brushed up against something.

"Look at this." I climbed down. Patch must have followed a path away from the main trail and he had brought us to an abandoned cabin. The roof was caved in on one side where a large tree had fallen over, but someone had lashed pine branches to cover the breach. The cabin was about the size of Mr. Dummond's hut by the river.

Patch nuzzled against me and I rubbed his nose and took off his saddle. "I wonder how far we came today Patch?" I tethered him near the doorway. "Probably no further than yesterday. At this rate, it'll take us a few more days to reach Richardson's Point."

I went inside and found there were more pine branches and two folded blankets in the corner, making a bed. Despite the damaged roof, the chimney and fireplace were intact with a couple of forked sticks fixed to use as a spit for roasting small game or hanging a pot over the fire. There were even a coffee pot, a cooking pot and a stack of wood on the hearth.

I wondered at first if the folks who owned the place would return, but quickly decided it didn't matter. I put the pots outside to collect rain water and started a fire with my flint. From my stash of food, I put two potatoes to cook in the ashes of the fire. Next I spread out my blanket and scarf so they would dry.

After a few minutes I blew on a potato and took a little bite, though it hadn't had time to cook properly. I'd left the door open to let in some light and I talked to Patch from where I was by the fire. "If it's raining tomorrow, I think we should stay here." Patch seemed to agree as he dipped his head and whinnied softly.

I used my borrowed blankets and lay with my back against the wall and my head on the picking bag. It was much warmer inside the cabin than it had been the night before in the lean to. And though it smelled a little of horse and wet blankets, I wasn't complaining. Still, I couldn't sleep. My blistered heels stung like fire. Finally, I could stand it no longer. By the flickering firelight, I took off my boots and slowly peeled off my socks. My heels were a sight. I used one of my socks to blot the blood away from open blisters. If only I had some salve. It was too cold to be barefoot, but I couldn't stand to put my boots back on either. I looked around until my gaze rested on the picking bag. I took out the largest piece of cloth—leftovers from making one of Pa's linen shirts by the look of it and tore off two long narrow strips.

I'd retrieved the pots and poured the water from the coffee pot into the cooking pot and set it to heat. There wasn't much but I dipped another scrap of cloth in it and used the hot water to clean my wounds. Then I wrapped and tied the long strips of cloth around my heels. I squeezed the water out of my socks and laid them near the fire to dry. That would have to do until morning.

Chapter 13

The rain continued on and off through the night and the next day. I used the time to dry as many things as I could by the fire and to rest my feet. I made ashcakes. I ate some, fed one to Patch, and kept the rest for later. In the afternoon, I checked my heels. The blisters were scabbing over so I moved the bandages carefully.

The third day my heels didn't hurt as bad so I covered them with more strips of cloth from the picking bag and pulled on my socks. My cough had eased as well. At dusk, the rain stopped and I slept soundly with high hopes for the morrow.

I woke when it was light and put on my boots. I gathered sticks and branches from the surrounding area to replace what I'd used and put everything back how I'd found it in the cabin. I was rested and felt good. I hoped to catch up to the saints very soon. I saddled and mounted Patch and we made our way back to the main trail.

In late afternoon, the sky clouded over and the rain started in again. Before long my hat was soaked through and the rain was beginning to seep through my blanket. I tried to play the game of choosing a spot to walk to and after reaching the goal choosing another spot. But after reaching another bend in the trail and seeing nothing different before me, I let Patch stop. "I'm afraid I need to rest my backside." I climbed down and led Patch forward for a time.

My heels were still tender so I walked slowly. Later I climbed back into the saddle and kept going. "I'm getting mighty tired of this rain. Do you hear me, Patch? Just when things were looking up, the rain started in again. I figure we have near five miles to go before we reach Richardson's Point. I wish we were there now." I looked at Patch as if he understood. "This water dripping off my hat makes it darn hard to see where the potholes are. I apologize for that inappropriate word but the whole trail looks like one big mud hole."

I was tired of the rain. I wanted to reach the saints. I must catch up to them. I had an idea. I told Patch, "Let's run for it. We can't get any wetter and it'll make it so we catch up to the saints faster." I kicked Patch hard with my heels and he jumped forward. I leaned close to his head and encouraged him to keep moving until we were galloping through the rain. Patch seemed to be enjoying the run as much as I was.

"Wahoo!" I hollered, taking off my hat and waving it above my head. "Now we're getting somewhere."

We ran for a half mile or so, Patch jumping over and around the mud holes. But then he jumped and I felt him falter when we landed. He took a funny step and jerked beneath me.

"What the—" Patch let out a high pitched scream and went down hard on his knees, sending me flying over his head. I landed in the mud. Disgusted, I spit mud from my mouth. I realized that Patch was making a strange whinnying sound and I turned to look at him.

"Patch, what's wrong?" My horse was lying on his side, thrashing his legs. I slogged my way back through the mud. A horrible groan came from deep within Patch's throat and his ears were plastered back against his head. He thrashed his legs again and again, trying to stand.

Staying clear of his hoofs, I knelt close to his head and stroked his neck and shoulder. "Whoa, Patch. Calm down boy. Let's see what happened." Patch stopped moving at the sound of my voice. I studied his condition as best I could with him lying in the mud. Patch's right foreleg had a large bulge below his knee. I took off my scarf and draped it over Patch's head so he couldn't see. I talked soothingly to him and patted his shoulder. I ran my hand down his hurt leg but when I touched the bulge, Patch kicked out and let out a loud whinny.

"I'm so sorry, boy," I repeated again and again as I stroked his neck.

What had I done? My impatience had caused this problem. What was I going to do now? I needed Patch to stand up in order for me to have any chance to help him.

"Patch," My voice shook. "Let's get you up." I pushed on the saddle horn and Patch paddled his legs but he couldn't stand. "This can't be, Patch. You have to get up, boy. I need you to stand, my friend."

I retrieved my scarf and wrapped it around my hands. Then I went to Patch's other side and pulled on the saddle horn with all my strength until Patch finally struggled to his feet. He stood on three legs and rested his right hoof on the ground. He shook his head at me and whinnied. I breathed heavily and stepped back. I looked into my horse's eyes and saw fear and pain.

"Come on, boy. You can do it." I encouraged Patch to follow me. He sort of hopped forward one step but when he put weight on his right foreleg, he screamed and lowered himself back down in the mud. I looked at Patch's leg. The bones had shifted more and torn through the skin. It was no use. Patch's leg was broken bad and it was my fault.

I'd seen horses with broken legs before and knew there was only one thing to do. He couldn't walk on three legs and I couldn't let him suffer. With shaking hands I took Pa's rifle and the powder horn from the saddle. I matter-of-factly measured and poured black powder into the muzzle. I tapped the rifle's butt against the ground to settle the powder, carefully wrapped a ball, and rammed it down the bore. I pointed the rifle at Patch's head, cocked the gun, and tried to squeeze the trigger. But this was Patch, my loyal friend. How could I shoot him?

I gripped the gun tightly and went to my knees in the mud beside my struggling horse. Tears ran down my cheeks. I shut my eyes and for the first time in days, I prayed.

"Father in Heaven, I need Thy help. You know how I decided back in Nauvoo that I wanted to do things on my own. I wanted to be a man, but... I can't do this. It's my fault Patch is hurt and I can't help him now. Father, please help me do what's best."

I opened my eyes and looked at Patch. He'd stopped struggling and was lying still. His eyes now seemed to only plead for relief. I wiped my eyes on my sleeve, stood up, and leveled Pa's gun.

"Goodbye, Patch." I said and squeezed the trigger.

I sat in silence in a little stand of aspen trees, listening to the rain. I'd carried and dragged the saddle, saddlebags and picking bag just that far. What was I going to do now? I used my scarf to wipe the rest of the mud from my face and hands. I wiped mud from the saddle, the saddlebags, and everything else. Nothing got much cleaner. While I worked I talked aloud, though there was no one nearby to hear me.

"There's nothing left for it. I'll have to walk the rest of the way to Richardson's point. I can do it. It's only a few more miles. I'll leave most everything here and come back for it when I can. Only thing, I sure wish it would stop raining."

As if on cue, the rain slowed and within a few minutes it had stopped completely. I smiled a little. Maybe my luck had changed —or maybe God had heard me again.

I put the remainder of my food in the picking bag with Ma's bible and the scraps of cloth and slung it and my water pouch over my shoulder. Then I picked up the powder horn and Pa's gun and, without looking back, started walking west.

I didn't talk as I followed the trail and I was careful to avoid any standing water. I stopped when it was too dark to see, made a small camp with a fire to keep warm, and began walking again as soon as it was light.

On the seventh day from when I left Sugar Creek, I reached what must have been the saints' camp at Richardson's Point. I could see where many tents had been set up and livestock had grazed, but that was all. I leaned the butt of Pa's gun on the ground. "I don't believe this," I said aloud to no one.

"The saints have to stop moving or I'll never catch up to them."

Standing there alone, I considered my options. It was too far to walk back to Sugar Creek to find Aunt Caroline. I didn't know where the saints would stop next. And by the looks of the smothered campfires, I was still a day or two behind them. I picked up Pa's rifle and set my face to the west. I would catch up to the saints or die trying. At least it hadn't rained for a few days.

I shot a rabbit that day and a couple of prairie chickens the next day. I skinned them with my knife and roasted them over the fire. They tasted good after so many days without. Trouble was I used the last of the black powder.

In the evening of the tenth day, I made camp near a little stream and huddled near my small fire. I was tired of walking. My cough was worse. I was tired of sleeping outdoors. I was tired of being alone. I examined the bottom of my boots; they were wearing thin. My heels had finally stopped bleeding and developed calluses, but my feet still ached from walking. I'd eaten the last of my food the night before. I'd drunk only a little water all day, knowing if I drank too much on an empty stomach it would make me vomit. I couldn't go much farther. I had to catch up to the saints or find someone else to help me. There had to be folks–maybe a town–nearby.

I looked through the picking bag once again. There wasn't any food left. I thumbed through Ma's bible but didn't take the time to read anything. I fingered my flute gently. I'd avoided playing it since Nauvoo. Now I blew softly into it, playing Ma's hymn. The sound was gentle and soothing. Soon I was aware of nothing else. The music seemed to push away the darkness. I played until the cold made me stop. I put more branches on the smoldering ashes to build up the fire, pulled my blanket tighter around my shoulders and watched the twigs burn.

Thoughts came to my mind. I had avoided playing my music to keep from thinking about Ma, but playing it now had eased my longing. And just as I'd avoided my music, I'd avoided my prayers. I realized that for a time I'd let my hard feelings for Pa, my earthly father, affect my feelings for my Heavenly Father.

He had been there for me with Patch. I realized I must trust Him again. I got Ma's bible and read in the Gospels where the Lord said he was aware of everyone—even to the number of hairs on someone's head. That promise was for everyone, me included. I got on my knees and said a simple prayer. "Father, please help me find the saints. I pray in Jesus' name. Amen." Warmth flowed through my body and I knew God had heard me. I lay back with my head on the picking bag and drifted into a peaceful sleep.

The peaceful feeling didn't last. I woke the next morning to harsh reality. I was weak and cold. The thought of trying to catch up to the saints was overwhelming. I said another prayer for help and I realized when I finished that I wasn't as hungry as before my prayer. I smiled. The Lord was answering my prayers. I covered the remains of my fire with dirt, picked up my few belongings and walked along the trail.

Somewhere along the way, I'd started talking aloud again and continued the habit. "What I need is a miracle. That's all. William and I talked about asking for one. That is what I need all right. Miracles happen all the time in the bible. God sent a ram to Abraham so he wouldn't have to sacrifice Isaac. I'd like a ram to be stuck over in those bushes right now." I laughed.

"Now days we still have miracles—what with the healings and the river freezing overnight and me not feeling hungry this morning." I shifted the rifle to my other hand. "For my miracle, I want a wagon full of saints to stop by and give me food and a ride right on into the camp of Zion." The thought made me laugh again then I sobered. "But the Lord helps those who help themselves, according to Ma and Aunt Caroline, so I'll keep walking."

The sun was high overhead and I had gone only a few miles. I found I was walking slower and slower; I was just plain spent. I trudged up one more hill when suddenly before me lay a beautiful little valley. I shaded my eyes and looked down at a little town of a dozen or so houses. "Not a moment too soon," I muttered, and broke into a weary trot.

Chapter 14

The town was off the trail and farther away than it first appeared. It was late afternoon when I finally reached a dilapidated sign on the outskirts which proclaimed that I was entering the town of Barlowe. As I reached the first house, I raised my hand in greeting. Three children playing in the yard stopped what they were doing and hurried inside without talking to me. No one smiled or waved as I walked down the main street. Not a very friendly place, I thought as I headed for what looked like a general store. It was on the left, nearly the last building in town.

"Good afternoon," I said to the dark haired girl behind the counter. The girl looked about my age. Her hair was in one long braid and she wore a long sleeved white blouse and full length skirt. She smiled shyly. "Good afternoon. May I help you?"

A man stepped from an adjoining room. "What do you want?" he asked in a rough voice.

I was taken back. "I'm in need of some supplies, sir."

"Have you got money?" He was dressed as a shopkeeper with a tightly tailored coat, vest, and tie.

"I have a flute, would you trade?" I pulled it from the picking bag.

"We don't trade that kind of merchandise," the man replied, eyeing me suspiciously.

"How about this rifle?" I held it out. "Would you trade for it?"

"Not with you," the man said curtly.

"Please sir," I said, "I came upon trouble some miles back."

"What does that matter to me?" The man leaned on the counter.

"You see, my horse fell and broke his leg."

"We still don't make trades with your kind," the man said with a scowl.

"Then perhaps," I said, "you might know where I could find work. I know how to—"

"Stop right there," the man interrupted and wagged his finger at me. "There's no work here for the likes of you."

"Surely I could do something," I pleaded. "I must look a sight, I know, but I'm not a thief or a bad person."

"You're one of them Mormons, though,

aren't you?" the man demanded.

"Yes, I'm Mormon." I stood up straighter. "What difference does that make?"

"Your people been coming through here plenty the last couple of weeks."

"How long ago was the last group here?" I interrupted.

"Not near long enough!" The man came around the counter and I took a step backward. "Some of them wanted help, too. The folks here in town decided we don't want Mormons coming here and taking over things. We made us a rule. We give no charity and no work to Mormons. So if you aren't a cash-paying customer, you better get yourself out of here." The man pointed to the door.

For a moment I stood still, staring at him. Then I took a deep breath and lifted my chin. "Sorry to have bothered you, sir. Good afternoon." I walked to the door and glanced back at the dark haired girl. She looked as if she'd like to say something to me, but the man took her by the arm and propelled her into the back room.

I walked out of the store and down the street in a kind of daze. I'd thought this town was the answer to my prayers, but I was wrong. All I wanted to do now was get away as quick as possible.

I made my way out of town toward the trail. No one spoke to me or looked as if they noticed I was there. Then as I passed the last house, I felt the sting of something hit my shoulder and I turned around. A boy about seven years old crouched behind a white picket fence with another rock in his hand. "Get out of here!" he hollered at me.

My blood boiled and I took a step toward him. But a woman ran out from the house, picked up the boy from behind and hurried him into the house. I clenched my fist. What was wrong with these folks? I hadn't done anything to any of them. With great effort, I walked away. I would choose to ignore their mean behavior. With my head held high and my back straight, I walked until no one from town could possibly see me, and then I began to run.

I ran and ran. I kept going as fast as I could until I thought my lungs would burst. I began to cough and stumbled over some loose rocks. Bushes seemed to reach out to grab me. I gasped for breath but I kept on running. When tears stung my eyes, I brushed them away. I couldn't stop until I was far away from that wretched town. I paid no attention to where I put my feet; I only wanted to get away. I stumbled again and cried out in pain as I crashed down onto my left knee. I'd lost my hat and landed in a heap in a little gully, the rifle and picking bag flung away. I lay there for a while venting my anger and pain.

After a while, I sat up to survey the damage. My left pant leg was ripped and my knee was already swollen and turning purple with a bloody gash. My left ankle was twisted and hurt when I touched it and my right palm was scratched and bleeding.

"Why is this happening to me?" I asked aloud. I scooted to where Pa's rifle lay and gingerly stood up using it as a crutch. I limped my way over to get the picking bag and then went back the way I'd come to look for my hat. I found it and slid down against the thin trunk of an aspen tree. What was I going to do now?

Unbidden, Aunt Caroline's words to Uncle David came back to my mind, "God's people have always been tried. It's after the trial that the blessings come. He will provide a way." The words felt like a sign. I thought about what they meant while I rested my leg. The Lord expected folks to do their best through their trials and then He'd bless them. I had done my best so far —I'd done all I could do by myself—and it wasn't enough.

I needed help. I needed God to provide a way. Carefully, I eased onto my one good knee. I closed my eyes and prayed. "Father in Heaven, it's me, Ammon. I need help again." An insect buzzed around my head but I didn't open my eyes. "I've done all I can to help myself, Lord. I'm alone now and I have nowhere to turn. I'm hungry, tired, sick, and I can barely walk."

I concentrated as hard as I could, willing God to hear my prayer. "I tried to get help in that town, Lord. But the man at the store wouldn't trade with me and I don't have any money. I'd have worked for food, but those folks wouldn't hire me. I'm trying to do what's right, to find the saints and follow the

Brethren. Maybe it was a bad idea to come by myself, but I'm here now, Lord. What can I do?"

I paused for breath. "I have faith in Thee. I know Thou canst help me, if it is Thy will. If not... then I still have faith that whatever happens is Thy will." With those words, I felt a warm surge in my chest and knew for sure that I did have faith. I kept praying, "Heavenly Father, I put my life in Thy hands. Please Lord, help me. I say this in the name of Jesus Christ, Amen."

I stayed where I was with my eyes squeezed shut for several long minutes. There was no voice from heaven. No angels appeared. No rescuing saints came by, but I did begin to feel a bit better. The warm feeling I had grew and filled that empty place that had been inside me. I knew it was because Heavenly Father had heard my prayer. I didn't know if He'd provide food, but that didn't matter because I knew I wasn't alone anymore. I leaned back against the tree and tried to think of what my next step should be.

Suddenly, the most direct thought came into my mind: Ammon, look in the picking bag for help.

What? I pulled my blanket over my head and quickly spread it on the ground. This was crazy. Look in the picking bag? There wasn't anything of worth in the picking bag. I'd sold the buttons, used most of the cloth, and eaten all the food. Still, the thought had been as real as if someone had spoken the words directly to me. I turned the picking bag upside down and shook it. My flute, Ma's bible and the last few pieces of cloth fell out. There was nothing more.

Disappointed, I wadded up the picking bag and flung it to the ground by my feet. As it hit, a glint caught my eye and something rolled out. I scooted over and reached for the shiny object. I held it up in the fading light. "A dollar?" I could hardly believe my eyes. A silver dollar had rolled out of the picking bag.

I whooped, coughed, hollered, and danced around on my good leg. Then I sat back down exhausted but exhilarated. Ma's bible lay open on the ground facedown. I picked it up, turned it over and tilted it to the remaining light. Ma had underlined a passage in St. Matthew. It read: *And all things, whatsoever ye shall ask in prayer, believing, ye shall receive.*

This was the faith Ma and Aunt Caroline had talked about. I knew it now for myself. I slowly knelt back up on my good knee, bowed my head and said, "Lord, I Thank Thee for answering my prayer." Then I added in a whisper, "You saved me!"

Chapter 15

Before the sun rose above the horizon the next morning, I started to walk back to Barlowe. Sometimes I used Pa's rifle as a crutch, which helped a bit. I shivered in the cold air. Every muscle and joint in my body complained as I limped along the trail. When I'd left the warmth of my little camp that morning, the excitement of the silver dollar dulled. I was mighty thankful for the miracle, but it hadn't changed the fact that I was cold, hungry and my leg hurt. I said my morning prayers, forced myself to wash in a small stream, and drank some water. As I hobbled along the trail, I kept repeating the words, "God helps those who help themselves."

After finding the dollar the night before, I had determined that for my part I had to walk back to Barlowe, buy some food, and then keep walking until

I caught up to the saints. I pulled my blanket tighter, adjusted my water pouch, jammed my hat farther down on my head and limped toward that hateful town.

Soon I saw the outline of buildings up ahead. I watched cautiously as I walked past the house where the boy had thrown the rock at me. I was nervous, but there wasn't any movement within or without the houses I passed. It was just a sleepy little town. I made my way cautiously toward the general store. I prayed that the owner would be nicer today. I almost turned back when I caught my first glimpse of the store, but I had to get food in order to do my part.

I took a deep breath and went inside. The dark haired girl was behind the counter. Her hair was in two long braids tied with yellow ribbons and she wore a clean apron over her long calico dress.

"Hello again." She smiled as she rearranged the jars on the counter.

"Hello." I took off my hat and stifled a cough.

"I felt bad when you left yesterday," she said. "Uncle was unkind. That's his way with strangers."

I cleared my throat and ran my hand through my straggly hair. "No real harm done, Miss."

"My name is Grace," she said pleasantly.

"Grace," I repeated. I could feel the color begin to rise in my cheeks. "My name is Ammon Blakeslee."

"I'd trade with you, Ammon. But if Uncle

found out . . . ." She glanced furtively over her shoulder. She came around the counter and crouched down so she couldn't be seen from the back room. She motioned for me to join her. "What happened to your knee?"

"I fell into a gully and hurt it, but I'll be alright," I said softly as I sat down beside her. "I need some food and then I'll be on my way. Your uncle made it clear that he wouldn't trade with me. But I have money now." I held the silver dollar up to show her. "I can buy food."

"How did you come by that?" she asked.

I showed Grace the picking bag and told her what had happened. Her eyes got big. "I'll help you for sure. I've never been part of a miracle before, but I always knew they could happen. Wait here while I make sure Uncle is still asleep. He came in real late last night."

I nodded and waited. Grace returned and beckoned for me to follow her. "We need to hurry. I'll give you the best prices I can."

Within a few minutes, I had a full water pouch, a sack and the picking bag filled with turnips, potatoes, carrots, onions; small packets of flour, salt and sugar; a chunk of dried meat, and two loaves of bread. Also, I had a small tin of ointment that Grace insisted on giving me for my knee and a tonic for my cough. I thanked her warmly and held out the silver dollar.

"I'll always remember you, Ammon." She

took the coin and hugged me quick, pressing her cheek against mine. "The Mormon boy with the miracle dollar."

"I'll remember you too. Thank you for your help. Maybe we'll meet again some day."

"I'd like that." Grace smiled, and her blue eyes shone.

I ate a hunk of bread and drank some water as I limped my way out of town. It was funny how the road didn't seem as rough to me now. Birds were singing and there were flowers—crocuses in bloom that I hadn't noticed before. It was a beautiful day! My thoughts turned to Grace. I'd liked the feel of her cheek on mine. I hoped we would meet again.

As I went, my thoughts raced over all of the things that had happened to me in the last few months. I hoped Sariah and Jacob were getting on well with Grandmother and Doctor Granger. I was sure that Heavenly Father would look out for them as I was sure He would provide for Uncle David, Aunt Caroline, and their new baby in New York. I thought of Ma next and wondered if she was watching over me from heaven. That made me smile. I wondered if she had anything to do with my miracle.

Then I thought of Pa. Things had certainly changed since Pa left on his mission. I wondered where he was now and what he'd do if he finally got back to Nauvoo and found we were gone. I had a pang of regret that he'd be all alone. In that instant, I realized my feelings toward him had changed. I didn't hate Pa anymore. He'd hurt me, true, but I wasn't angry with him anymore. Instead, I felt only sadness for what had happened.

I camped for two days in the same place I had the night before. I fixed up my knee with the ointment from Grace and the last strips of cloth from the picking bag. I sewed up the hole in my pants. I made ashcakes and vegetable stew and rested so I would be able to continue my journey. In the evenings, I said my prayers, played my flute and looked at the stars.

After breakfast the following day, I limped determinedly forward following the ruts left by the wagons that had gone ahead. I covered several miles and made camp by a stream for the night. I could feel in my heart that I was getting close to the saints. On the third day from my camp near Barlowe, I noticed what looked like smoke up ahead. I strained my eyes to see better and it was true. I kept walking and soon I could see a group of tents and wagons. It had to be the saints. I whooped and hollered and waved my hat as I hurried forward.

The camp was large and spread out over a large area. By nightfall, I'd asked around and made my way past many campsites and families until in the distance I saw the familiar black felt hat of my friend.

"William!" I called loudly.

William looked up and saw me. A smile

spread across his face. "Ammon!" He raced toward me. "What happened to you? You look awful!"

I laughed, "I made it here just the same."

"That you did, my friend. That you did." William took my bag and rifle and I leaned on his arm and limped into his family's camp. Soon we were surrounded by his family members. I was hugged and pounded on the back. I had found the saints at last.

A few days later, William and I were sitting on a log by the fire. I had begun to whittle another flute and was, once again, telling him about my adventures on the flatboat. A man rode into camp on a horse. The chestnut looked familiar to me—like one owned by Brother Matthews, Pa's missionary companion. I couldn't see the man's face very well because his hat was pulled low, but I knew him by the way he sat. I stood up and waved.

"Ammon? Is that you?" the man called.

"Yes sir. It sure is me." I smiled up at my father.

Pa was off his horse in a second and hurrying to me. His clothes were worn and he'd lost weight. But it was Pa's strong arms hugging me and his voice in my ear. "Finding you, son, is the answer to my prayers."

"The answer to mine, too," I whispered as I hugged Pa back.

"I had to buy a new hat a few months ago

when I lost mine," Pa laughed a little. "And Brother Matthews lent me his horse since you had Patch."

"I'm sorry I caused so much trouble."

Pa and I sat by the fire and William excused himself to care for Brother Matthews' horse.

"I got back to Nauvoo a week ago," Pa explained. "Caroline and David were living in the old house there. They told me about your ma." His voice trailed and I could see pain in his eyes as he said, "Your ma's death is the harshest of blows to me, Ammon. I'm so sorry I wasn't there when she needed me, when the rest of you needed me."

I nodded but kept silent.

"Caroline told me you left Sugar Creek to join the saints. She said you wanted to go alone and she and David figured you would make it to this camp within a few days."

"It took a while longer," I said. "But with God's help I made it." Then I told Pa about my journey. He listened quietly asking a question here and there.

When I'd finished Pa put his hand on my shoulder and cleared his throat. "I'm proud of you, Ammon. You've become a man while I was away."

"Yes, sir," I said simply.

"Pa," I said after a few minutes. "Ma had me promise to tell you something. She wanted you to know she loved you, and . . . so do I."

Pa smiled and hugged me. "I love you too, son."

"Now," he continued, "I must go report on my mission to the Brethren. Then you and I can make plans to fetch Sariah and Jacob from your grandmother. That is, if you want to go with me to Connecticut. Now that you're grown, I expect you'll make your own decisions."

I let Pa's words sink in. I had grown up while he was away, and, more importantly, I had learned that with God's help I could do anything. "I'll come with you I said."

Later that night, I looked up at the stars and thought about the day. Pa had returned to Nauvoo as he'd promised, even though it was later than we'd expected. Soon he and I would go to Connecticut to get Jacob and Sariah and then we would all rejoin the saints. I smiled and began to play my flute. I played Ma's hymn and felt the now familiar warmth fill my chest. I was reassured once again that Ma was all right. And I knew that someday, just as she had promised, we'd all be home together in heaven.

Epilogue

I never did give the picking bag back to Jacob. I offered it to him when Pa and I got to Connecticut, but he said to keep it. So I did. I had it when we visited Aunt Caroline, Uncle David, and their baby daughter, Jane. I had it when we rejoined the saints who had moved on to the Valley of the Great Salt Lake. When I was older and went on missions for the church, I took the bag with me. And when my wife, Grace, and I settled into our little brick home in northern Utah, the picking bag had a special place on our bookshelf. I'd take it down now and then to show our children and grandchildren. They never tired of hearing about the miracle and I never tired of telling about it.

Acknowledgements

Thank you to the myriad of people who helped me with this book. Starting with Mary Ryan, my teacher and mentor from The Institute of Children's Literature (ICL), who first read and critiqued *The Picking Bag*, and later introduced me to the Northern Ohio Society of Children's Book Writers & Illustrators (SCBWI). Thanks to all my Ohio writing friends, and critique group partners. (You know who you are.) Thanks also to my Utah writing friends Carol Lynch Williams, Rick Walton, and the gang from the Writing & Illustrating for Young Readers Conference (WIFYR). Special thanks go to Sandra Warren, Gretchen Griffith, Tom Sjoerdsma and Margaux Kent, for without their help this book would never have been published. And finally, a huge thank you to my family, who gives me endless support, and to my husband, who is the love of my life, my best friend, and my biggest fan.

The Picking Bag is fiction. However, the miracle of the silver dollar is inspired by a true story from my family history of Caroline Francis Angell Davis Hollbrook, which probably took place somewhere in Utah after 1850. For literary purposes, I moved the story to the Nauvoo period and arranged for Ammon to be alone despite the fact that there were thousands of Mormons moving west in 1846.

About the Author

Debbra Beecher Nance was born and raised in the state of Washington, and later lived in Virginia, Ohio, and Utah. She and her husband currently live in a little hollow in Taylorsville, Utah, where she loves to read, write, and have her children and grandchildren visit.

Made in the USA
Charleston, SC
29 January 2016